Darcy *and* *the* Duchess

MARY ANNE MUSHATT

ISBN: 0984262105
ISBN-13: 9780984262106

This entire process would not have happened without the support and understanding of my family and friends. In particular I would like to thank my husband, David and our sons, John and Jacob, for their patience and understanding. To my sisters Ginny and Kim thank you for your unrelenting love and encouragement. To the women who undertook the arduous task of brainstorming ideas and then refining them throughout the writing of this story, thank you. Nina Benneton and tJean are legendary in the Jane Austen fan fiction world and my debt to them is great. I would also like to thank all who have read my work and sent encouraging words that gave me the strength and confidence to continue.

Thank you.

~ PROLOGUE ~

November, 1809
Vienna, Austria

Elizabeth tapped her foot on the pebbles of the walkway in the magnificent park. The Josepburg was an oasis as well as *the* premier site in Vienna to see and be seen by the fashionable, during the day. Yet now, after waiting for nearly an hour, the young lady noted that shadows were gathering as evening approached. The late autumn air chilled and Elizabeth wanted to return to the hotel, but she had promised her uncle to wait for him there. And, she had to confess, the convoluted path Fraulein Hallgrogh had taken to the park had skewed her sense of direction. Her German was good, but it was getting dark, and she felt fear nipping at her heels. While the nannies and young mothers had been about Elizabeth had felt safe, but evening was approaching, the park emptying, and daylight was dimming into lengthening shadows. Turning her collar against the breeze she scanned the entranceway for the familiar face of her uncle.

"Miss Elizabeth? Miss Elizabeth Bennet?" a voice cut through her thoughts. It took a moment for her to realize the voice spoke in English. She turned toward the decidedly British accent, finding a man of about twenty five coming towards her, her name on his lips. She looked to him and smiled. He felt his world brighten.

"Miss Elizabeth Bennet?" he asked after jogging over to her. His eyes danced in delight.

"Yes, I am she," she offered, assessing his character by his appearance and what he would say and do next.

"Excellent!" He said, bending over at the waist in response to his ramshackle run. "You must forgive me, I am... it seems my fencing master is right... I *am* out of shape!" He laughed and Elizabeth felt herself relax enough to enjoy his merriment.

"Whom do I have the pleasure of addressing, sir? Tell me quickly, before you expire in a heap before me!"

A dark look crossed his face and she was shaken by his intensity. Before thinking she touched his arm, her eyes seeking forgiveness. He looked up to see her deep brown eyes still sparkling with emotion. He saw an understanding that her words may have offended. He was struck by her awareness and caring towards a complete stranger that fate had set in her path.

"Miss Elizabeth... Miss Bennet," the man said, straightening to his full height. At nearly six feet he towered over the petite, dark haired woman, and she took a step back. "Your Uncle Gardiner, Edward Gardiner has sent me after you."

The surprise on her face tickled him, and he tried to restrain from chuckling outright. 'This is the most singular reaction I have *ever* received from an Englishwoman! Any woman, come to think of it.'

"And?" she continued. "For what purpose did he send you?"

"Why to collect you from the cold of the night, milady." He offered his arm but she resisted. He looked at her, then looked again. Recalling the words of her uncle the charmed man said, "He bade me tell you 'Sweet Kate, I bid you welcome.' I confess I thought him a bit daft, since he assured me your name is Elizabeth, not Katherine, but by the transformation of your countenance I assume it is a code, or some such."

"Indeed, sir. While visiting a foreign capital it is wise to have a method of deciphering friend from foe."

He looked on as she took his arm in hers indicating that he should lead on. Traversing the park in the increasing cold, Elizabeth gleaned that her uncle had met an old friend and their conversation had delayed him. "Rather than disturb their reunion, I volunteered to come and fetch you."

"Like a hound, sir?"

"Coming for his treasure," he smiled back at her and she laughed at the delight in his eyes.

"Oh, you are someone to watch, kind sir," she said as they entered the lobby where her uncle conversed with a man in his late thirties, wearing spectacles.

"Elizabeth!" exclaimed the impeccably attired Edward Gardiner. In his early forties, Mr. Gardiner took in his relative's appearance and immediately approached his adventurous niece. "But where is Fraulein Hallgrogh?" Concern permeated his entire being, impressing the younger man sent to find the errant Miss Bennet.

With a roll of her eyes, Elizabeth answered, "She found a gaggle of her friends and went off to some tea room or other."

"I am sorry, my dear. I am most seriously displeased." Turning to her companion, Mr. Gardiner continued. "Thank you, your Grace. I am doubly grateful to you. I had no idea Fraulein Hallgrogh was so unreliable."

"Your Grace?" Elizabeth's eyebrow cocked inquisitively.

"Forgive me, I… my manners were completely overcome by..." he stammered for words that would not reveal how taken he was by her. "… the liveliness of your tongue." He winced as both the gentlemen and the older woman who had joined them all eyed him suspiciously.

"Hmmm," was all Elizabeth could say, although she observed the gentleman with an assessing eye. "I believe I recognize a bit of flattering fluff when I hear it, your Grace." The last was said with exaggeration dripping off every syllable.

Mr. Gardiner relaxed at the ease with which Elizabeth handled herself. He knew that if anything was amiss, she would convey it instantly. As she was at ease, alert, a playful smile on her open face, he surmised her enjoyment with the banter her new acquaintance provided. "Elizabeth? May I properly introduce Lord Rafael Gainsbridge, the Duke of Deronshire and his aunt, her Grace, Lady Agatha Pembroke, Duchess of Leicester and Dr. Alford Grimwald, a university colleague of mine."

Genuinely impressed with the ease she felt with these exalted personages, Elizabeth curtsied first to the older woman, and then to the gentlemen. "Your Grace, doctor."

His Grace chuckled at her blush while her ladyship surveyed how her nephew's eyes never left the face of this enchanting young woman. Looking over she caught Mr. Gardiner's eye, enjoying the twinkle she found there.

"Mr. Gardiner, my nephew and I are weary of our desultory company. Will not you and your niece join us for dinner?"

Assessing the blush creeping across Elizabeth's cheek, he consented willingly. "We would be most obliged, your Grace."

"Yes, thank you, your Grace," added Elizabeth in almost a whisper.

"Dame Agatha," enjoined the young Duke, a smile playing upon his lips. Taking a look at his timepiece, he exclaimed, "It is now five o'clock! Shall we say eight? Here in the lobby?"

"Will that grant you enough time, Elizabeth?" Edward Gardiner asked, impertinently.

Blushing even more furiously, Elizabeth looked at her uncle, the tease in his eye. Taking a quick glance at their companions, she replied, "Yes, Uncle, I believe I may complete my transformation from street urchin to lady in three hours! Will that give you ample time, sir?" All chuckled over this.

"We will have to see, now, will we not?" he asked, innocently. "We must make haste then. I need every moment to arrange my coiffure!" They all laughed outright. Before Mr. Gardiner and his niece headed off towards their rooms, they bid Dr. Grimwald goodnight as he was headed off for a night at the opera. When their three companions were out of sight, Dame Agatha turned to her nephew.

"And you, Rafe, will that give *you* enough time?"

Fatigue registering in his eyes, he replied, "Yes, Agatha. I will rest and take care." Meeting her raised brow he added, "Do not fret, dear heart. I will take a hot bath as well." He took her arm and they too, headed for their suite. "I believe an evening in the delightful company of Miss Bennet will take away the chill," adding in his mind, 'the one that has rested in my heart for so very long.'

~

January, 1810
Glen Morrow
County Kildare, Ireland

Fitzwilliam Darcy read the letter in his hand for the third time. 'Rafael Gainsbridge in love! Who would have ever thought it?! And to a country lass, at that! Singular.' He looked into the fire blazing before him, wondering who this creature could be to convince an even more confirmed bachelor than himself, to marry. 'Perhaps it is time to return to England,' he thought, 'and see what he is about before he goes and makes a horrendous mistake.'

Although the Duke of Deronshire was no one's fool, Darcy still believed an objective appraisal was necessary, especially in matters as delicate as the heart. 'What if she has forced his hand?' he thought, remembering how persuasive some women could be. 'Certainly his position in society would be incentive enough, but then there is his fortune. And since the death of his parents he has been adrift. I should have invited him to Ireland with me. It would have been nice to have his company and advice in settling this matter. Rafe always had a good head for business. Although I presume there is no chance he would leave his,' he checked the letter again for her name, 'Miss Elizabeth Bennet, in order to help an old friend. No,' he chuckled. 'I do believe Rafe is about to get his leg shackled and there is nothing I can do about it.'

Nevertheless, Fitzwilliam Darcy of Pemberley of Derbyshire, and Glen Morrow of County Kildare began what turned out to be lengthy preparations for his return to London.

~ CHAPTER ONE ~

February, 1810
London

When Elizabeth and Mr. Gardiner returned to London, she had no expectations that the Duke would continue his suit. She was surprised, therefore, when he requested and received permission to court Elizabeth first from the lady herself, and then Edward Gardiner, her guardian in London. Her father was duly invited to town, as Elizabeth and her relations felt it was still too early in the relationship to expose the Duke and Duchess to Mrs. Bennet and her enthusiasm.

Therefore, in the last week of February Rafael Gainsbridge knelt before Elizabeth Bennet in the parlor of her Cheapside relations, prepared to utter the immortal words, "I love you, Elizabeth. I will love you forever. Will you marry me?"

So great was her shock that she stuttered for the first time in her life, until she recovered use of her tongue. Pulling him off his knee and onto the sofa with her,

Elizabeth held his hand and looked into his eyes. "Are you... are you sure, Rafe?"

"You question my devotion?" he asked, his eyes hopeful.

"I question your sanity! We..."

"You do not love me?"

"It is not that!" He looked at her, not allowing her to look away.

"Then tell me, what is it?"

"You do not know my family... They can be..."

"Elizabeth, I am not marrying your family. I wish to spend the remaining time I have on this earth, with you, my dearest." He squeezed the hands he held. "You do not know the joy you bring me, simply by allowing me to be near you, to look into your eyes, to see your smile, to hear the incredibly witty words that emerge from your delectable lips." Here he licked his own while focusing on hers. Elizabeth felt her heart pound, her blood race and her lips itch.

"Yes, Rafe, I will marry you," she whispered, knowing for certain that she returned his love.

Elizabeth's breath was taken away as Rafe pressed his lips to hers. Their softness astounded her as she felt more than just skin touching skin. When his lips parted and his tongue touched her she felt his love enter her, embrace her, and his arms wrap around her waist, pulling her to him. When their lungs required air, he pulled away to whisper, "My darling," then crushed her to him. With her ribs pressed against him, she felt confusion when his body recoiled, as if he had been punched. She pulled back, her eyes searching for an answer.

When he had regained his composure, he looked up into her eyes and knew his day of reckoning had come. He removed his arms from her waist to clasp her hands. She waited patiently for him to speak.

"Elizabeth…"

"Yes, Rafael?" Her eyebrow quirked and he knew his hour of truth had come.

"I intended to speak to you about this, before we… before I go and speak to your father… about our marriage. I hope you will forgive me the hubris of asking for your hand before I tell you…"

"Tell me what, your Grace?" Elizabeth's formality indicated she felt he was toying with her.

Fearing what was to come, he steeled himself for her rejection. "When we met, I was not in Vienna on *business*." He watched with a sickening sense of dread as she withdrew her hands to clasp them in her own lap. He soldiered on. "No, although never actually claiming that business brought me to the continent, both Agatha and I were content to let one and all think so." Elizabeth waited, her fingers tapping in succession on her arms, now folded across her chest. "Yes," he continued, taking in her growing agitation. You recall our first meeting?" She nodded. "That Dr. Grimwald was present?" She nodded again, concern growing in her eyes as she started adding the facts into a most unpleasant summation. She looked at him with fear. "Dr. Grimwald is my personal physician, and it was his recommendation that we traverse the continent as soon as it was safe, to seek the Dasweiller clinic. Grimwald was aware of a Dr. Frankelstone who has new ideas on the treatment of…" he looked away briefly. "Of cancer."

Elizabeth gasped as the Duke barely whispered this last word. Her hands flew from her arms to his, but Rafael refused to look directly into her eyes. "I do not want your pity, Elizabeth."

"You do not have my pity, Rafael. You have my heart. I love you! And I will stand by you, no matter what."

He looked at her as profound joy radiated throughout his body, supplementing his blood and he embraced her again. "Truly, my dearest darling? You will still marry me?"

"Of course, Rafael. Why would I not?"

He pulled back, holding her arms in his hands. His demeanor and voice were completely serious. "Because it is incurable. The end… will be… unseemly."

She read his seriousness carefully before responding. "I thank you for the opportunity to renege and save myself. But I would be miserable wasting any more precious time without you, Rafael. I am yours."

He kissed her passionately, and she returned it completely before they broke apart and he went in search of Mr. Bennet.

∾

Lady Agatha made the rounds of society introducing Elizabeth to her friends and the notables she felt it essential for Elizabeth to meet. All were taken by the charm and poise of the unknown young woman who would soon rise to the pinnacle of society. Her beauty and virtues were extolled in every salon, every men's club, and on the floor of the premier balls of that season. The salons were abuzz with excitement at the elegant trousseaux the future Duchess had chosen. All were pleasantly surprised at how doting the Duke had become. Of course, there were the disappointed matrons and young women who had counted on his title and fortune to bolster their own. Then there were others whose outrage stemmed from the fact that Miss Elizabeth Bennet was not of their ilk, only the daughter of a poor country gentleman, and, they were sure, would demean the house of Gainsbridge. But the Duke was known for a keen wit and intelligence, and all too often, these same ladies who had coveted his place in society had been at the biting end of it. They mourned the loss of his fortune and connection, but not of the man.

Three weeks before the early April wedding, a caravan of carriages made its way out of London toward Hertfordshire. The Duke had leased the nearby estate of Netherfield for his friends and relations to witness his marriage to Elizabeth Bennet. Those in attendance were the Fitzwilliams with their niece Georgiana Darcy, the Duncasters, Lord Edwin Aubrey, cousin of Lady Agatha, and one Dr. Alfred Grimwald. While all wondered about *his* inclusion, most assumed he was welcome in case Dame Agatha, as she was affectionately known, would require his services.

There were teas, dinners and balls celebrating the happy couple, who had precious little time alone. As the day of the ceremony approached, Colonel Fitzwilliam rode into Meryton. Colonel Fitzwilliam had been a family friend for years, spending many summers with his cousin, Fitzwilliam Darcy, and the Duke. He was curious about meeting the future Duchess, and the charming array of sisters that Rafe had promised.

Two nights before the wedding, the Duke hosted a ball at Netherfield for gentry and peer alike. Elizabeth was resplendent in a gown of persimmon red silk, rubies around her neck and dangling from her ears. Red and white crystals sparkled in her auburn tresses, which were neatly piled upon her head. Happiness radiated throughout her entire being, and as she stepped through Netherfield's door her eyes searched for her betrothed.

Rafael Gainsbridge led his fiancée to the first set, and all eyes fixed both on her beauty and the joy emanating from her intended. Even Mrs. Bennet had to stop crowing about her fortune and the unbelievable luck of becoming the mother of a duchess, to marvel at the transformation of her second child, who, by chance, was her least favorite. The Gardiners were present, and were not sure which was the greater miracle, Mrs. Bennet's silence or the triumphant joy of their beloved niece.

Elizabeth fingered the gown hanging off her armoire. The delicate embroidery and bead work called for her touch. It was the gown she had dreamt of as a young girl when pressed by Jane to imagine her wedding day. For hours the girls would digress, imagining the finery of flowers, silk and lace. Well Jane would. Elizabeth often sat, her head cocked to the side trying to imagine who the person, the man waiting at the end of the aisle would be. 'Strange,' she thought, 'I had always thought him to be dark, like me.' She tilted her head to the other side as Rafael's blond head filled her mind. She saw his smile, the way his eyes danced, heard his quick wit engage her own in a duet of ideas. Remembering his words reminded her of his lips and how they felt pressed upon her own, as well as her hand, fingers, neck. 'I must stop this and prepare!'

To cool her thoughts, Elizabeth walked to the window, looking out as dawn's first light pierced the dispelling grey. 'It is hard to conceive that only six months ago I woke on a morning like this, preparing to meet my uncle in town and journey to the continent. Today, I prepare to meet my husband... my husband.' Suddenly the thought frightened her. 'This is forever! How am I to bind myself to him? I know so little of him, and he of me. How are we ever to...?' She pulled away from the cool glass, her arms wrapped around her.

'And he is ill.' She walked the length of her room. 'What will happen to me after... after he is gone? I will be alone in a world I am unfamiliar with, without Rafael to guide me... shield me from the *ton*. It was difficult enough with him by my side.' She flopped on her bed, puffing the down quilt all around her. She pulled her pillow to her chest, resting her head upon it.

'What then?' she asked, her fingers ticking at the pillow. "Agatha!" She looked up, immensely calmed by the thought. 'Agatha will stand by me, and perhaps by then there shall be a child, or two, or perhaps… more!' Her smile at this thought brought forth the love she felt for the man she was to marry. She was overjoyed that she had finally found a man, who was not her father or uncle, who enjoyed her sense of humor and encouraged her lively mind and curiosity about the world. Again, she recalled his kisses and how she felt within the embrace of his strong arms. 'And how do I feel? Protected for sure, but there is more, something else, something that sends my blood racing when he pulls me to him.' Elizabeth felt free and the desire to feel more of him. At first overcome with the wantonness of the sensation, she had quickly grown comfortable with his nearness, finding herself craving the stolen moments when they could be alone. With these thoughts warming her heart and bringing color to her cheek her beloved sister found her, signaling it was time to prepare and meet the day.

Later that morning, Rafael Gainsbridge, Duke of Deronshire, pledged his love and troth to Elizabeth Bennet, of Longbourn. There was nary a dry eye in the church as they exchanged their vows. Lady Agatha, sitting in the front pew, Georgiana Darcy at her side, was beaming with joy. Georgiana, so unused to such unbridled emotion marveled at the transformation created by the woman standing at the altar with her brother's sardonic friend.

'Rafael looks happy,' she thought. Looking at Dame Agatha, who had become a surrogate grandmother, Georgiana noticed the unmistakable approval and conviction with which the older woman witnessed the nuptials. The only time the older woman's face showed pain was when the Duke proclaimed he would love Elizabeth until 'death do us part.'

~

After a bountiful reception held at Netherfield, the newlywed couple made haste to London for their first night together. The rest of the wedding party remained in Hertfordshire, not feeling the same urgency to depart.

~

The wedding night of the Duke and Duchess of Deronshire was cold outside the walls of their London townhouse. Within, however, was a different story altogether. The young duchess sat in her dressing room in her nightgown, her skin warmed by the fire blazing in the grate. She sat brushing her hair, her maid dismissed for the night long ago.

Both her mother and Aunt Gardiner had given their versions of what this night would bring, and she trusted and hoped it was her aunt who had the truth of it. 'At least Aunt and Uncle still speak to each other about more than the weather!' she thought as the hoar hair bristles of her brush slid through her hair.

"Elizabeth?" Rafael asked, his eyes opened wide to take in her beauty. He stood in the doorway, amazed at the woman who was now his wife. She turned toward him, standing as his gaze held her.

"Rafael," she said as calmly as she could, though her heart beat widely in her chest.

"Do you… I am not disturbing you?" he asked through a parched throat.

"No, Husband," she replied. They stood still, each drinking in the other, he in a dressing gown of cobalt silk contrasting with the pale ivory of his skin. She could see his breath was labored, a flush just overcoming his cheek. When her eyes met his, she saw that he was as overcome as she. So she did what felt natural to her opening her arms, an invitation he readily accepted.

Stepping into her embrace his face embedded in her hair, his arms pulled her to his body. She could feel his lungs expand and contract, and that he wore nothing beneath his robe. The heat from his hand, now running over her back seared, and she pulled her head back. His lips met hers, engulfing her in a kiss that transported her to a new world.

∾

The spring of 1810 was spent happily between the Gainsbridge estate, *Crystalglen* and London. When forced to London, the Duke and Duchess found ample amusement in the artists and philosophers in town. Rafe adored Elizabeth and enjoyed exposing her to the best minds of their time. They lived beneath the radar of society, skirting the teas and tableaux in favor of conversations with the creators of the art, literature and music of their age. The discussions were lively and intense with heated debate that more often ended amicably, but not always so.

Rafael's visits to Dr. Grimwald continued but he felt in his heart, his end approaching. He spoke with Dame Agatha who empathized, but could do little to soothe his soul. She, however, encouraged him to speak with Elizabeth.

~ CHAPTER TWO ~

April 1810
Wyndom House, London

Evening gathered in the shadows of the Master's chambers. The heaviness of winter had passed, leaving the possibilities of spring behind. Rafe and Elizabeth had spent the afternoon with a select group of friends discussing the latest works of Lord Byron. They had taken the carriage through the park for Elizabeth to enjoy the early blossoms. The air was fresh, cool, and it renewed their spirits. The winter had not been kind to Rafe. Elizabeth and Dr. Grimwald did their best to keep him comfortable, and to revive his spirits, but his stomach continued to give offense.

Elizabeth was in her chambers, preparing for a ball at Lord and Lady Granby's home. Rafe had taken his tonic and sat, alone in his room awaiting the promised relief to materialize. He pulled his chair to the window to sit overlooking the courtyard garden where Elizabeth had planted bulbs he had specially ordered from Holland. 'Will I be well enough to see their bloom?' he asked morosely, as his fingers stroked his chin. These dark thoughts were scattered by the sound of Elizabeth's laughter in the adjoining chamber. The sound recalled her joy she had working with Aimsley, their groundskeeper in London. Together they had overseen the planting of the bulbs that Rafe and Elizabeth had so artfully arranged through the long afternoons of winter on sheet after sheet of draftsman's paper. A smile overcame him as he recalled Elizabeth reading aloud to him. She fed his spirit with hope and the fire for survival. She was patient and kind, and her kisses ignited his passion for her flesh and for life. 'By God, I wish to live and love that woman!'

Meersham's entrance alerted him to the passage of time. His manservant lit the tapers before arranging the Duke's garb for the ball. Without much delay, Rafe was suitably attired in an elegant coat of indigo and matching breeches. His stockings were of the creamiest white and he looked every inch the elegant gentleman he was. When Meersham retreated, Rafael went to his desk and pulled out a velvet box. He opened it admiring the emeralds and diamonds he intended to place about Elizabeth's neck. Seized with the desire to see them upon her neck he advanced to the intervening door.

He knocked once and heard her call, "Enter." He pushed open the door and strode in to see his beloved rise and greet him. She held her arm out to him, but he could not move. 'Astounding!' he thought.

"Rafe, are you well?" Elizabeth asked, her smile turning to concern.

Rafael gathered what remained of his wits. "Yes, Elizabeth, I am. I am simply overcome by your beauty." She blushed becomingly. "Here, darling. I thought these might complement your gown, although nothing compares to you." He advanced, taking her in his arms to kiss. Their lips met and Rafael felt an explosion of sensation. Elizabeth held on to him as if she would fall, and he smiled knowing he was not alone in the overwhelming feelings created in the physicality they shared. Maria returned to her mistress as the master wound his hands through Elizabeth's hair. Her intake of breath alerted them to her presence and their obligation to attend the evening's festivities.

"I apologize, Maria," he said, looking all the while into Elizabeth's eyes. "For mussing the elaborate styling you have wrought with Elizabeth's hair." The Duke gently pulled one curl till it straightened, watching it bounce back when he released it. Elizabeth smiled at his playfulness.

Elizabeth addressed her maid with a smile. "Oh Maria, what am I to do with this husband?"

Maria blushed and quickly addressed the tussle of curls, re-pinning those that had escaped their bonds. The couple stood, hands clasped together. When she left, Rafael picked up the box he had deposited on the vanity. His eyes never leaving hers, he opened it for her approval.

She looked at the jewels then up at her husband. "Rafael! They are incredible!" Her hands clasped her cheek before she tentatively reached out to touch the co-joined stones.

"Will you wear them tonight, my love?" She nodded. "My father gave these to my mother soon after they were married, and I would so love to see them around your lovely neck."

She gazed at Rafael before throwing her arms around him. She whispered in his ear, "Rafael, thank you. I love you so!" He pulled back, juggling the open box and its contents. He then turned her around and removed the necklace from its case. Unclasping the jewels, he draped them around her neck, kissing the skin just above and below where the stones lay. He felt her shiver as his kisses touched her.

Elizabeth beheld herself in the mirror, her handsome husband standing behind gazing into her reflection. Her green gown of the finest silk complimented the stones she now wore. Rafael leaned forward, taking the ear bobs out from their case, handing them to his wife. Silently she fastened each to her ears, enjoying his fascination reflected back to her in the glass.

"You are beautiful, Elizabeth," he said, hoarsely. "I am indeed, a fortunate man."

∾

The grand hall glittered with crystal and candlelight, gleaming in the sheen of silk, satin and gems.

Eyes sparkled, and flirted, coyly leading some on, while others shied away, hidden. The ball had been underway for quite some time when the Duke and new Duchess of Deronshire arrived. They quickly made their way to Lord and Lady Granby who were just about to end the receiving line. "There you are, Rafe!" Lord Granby called out, catching sight of the Duke. Lady Granby held out her hand to him and he quickened his step to take hold and press a quick kiss to the back of her hand.

"Lady Amanda," he said, happy to be with his father's friends. "Allow me to present my lovely bride, Elizabeth." Rafael stepped back to bring forth Elizabeth, and Amanda smiled to see the son of her girlhood friend so happy with his unconventional choice. 'She is lovely,' Lady Amanda thought as did her husband, Thomas Granby.

Elizabeth smiled at Rafael, and Lord Granby caught his breath. 'Superb!' thought the older man, momentarily lost in recollections of years long gone, when beautiful women like the one before him, smiled at him.

"Enchanted," Lord Granby eked out when he roused himself from his thoughts. He saw the couple looking at him, and Elizabeth's eyebrow cocked provocatively, her eyes dancing with delight.

"Lady Granby, Lord Granby, a pleasure to finally meet you." Elizabeth said in a full voice.

"And you as well, your Grace. You look beautiful tonight," Lady Granby said smiling at her guest and her now blushing husband.

The Duke and Duchess made their way through the assembly, slowly meandering about the room until the music began. With a deep bow, Rafael addressed his wife. "Your Grace, if you are not otherwise engaged, may I have the honor of the first?"

Elizabeth giggled and curtsied her reply. "The honor is mine, my lord, as is the pleasure." With a grin that reached his eyes, the Duke of Deronshire led his bride to the floor, capturing all eyes as they took their place in the line.

Midway through the first set, Fitzwilliam Darcy entered the hall, accompanied by Charles Bingley, Miss Caroline Bingley and Mr. and Mrs. Stephen Hurst. Caroline Bingley was positively glowing to be seen on the arm of the dashing Mr. Darcy, while every one else in her party only looked annoyed at their rude and tardy arrival.

Darcy disengaged himself in search of his cousin, Richard Fitzwilliam, leaving Caroline to finally notice that no one had paid her entrance any heed. As he walked the perimeter of the room, Darcy glanced about at the dancers. His eye latched on to a woman dancing. Her smile warmed him even from across the room. She turned and he was struck by the way her joy reached her eyes. 'My God, she is beautiful!' he thought in wonder. 'I must meet her!' and he moved to keep her in his sights. His excitement paled when he noticed her partner and the way the couple regarded each other. "Rafael!" he said aloud, crestfallen to recall the Duke's recent marriage to a country nobody with no fortune and few connections.

"Darcy! There you are!" Colonel Richard Fitzwilliam boomed, slapping his younger cousin on the back. Darcy nearly stumbled forward at the unexpected blow. "Do not tell me one of the debutantes has caught your eye at last." Fitzwilliam continued.

"Fear not. Tell me, Richard, who dances with Rafael?"

Richard looked around at the dancers until he found his friend. "That, cousin, would be the lovely Elizabeth Gainsbridge, Duchess of Deronshire, the Miss Bennet that was."

"Ah," sighed Darcy.

"Yes. That appears to be the reaction of all our male friends when they discover her identity." Lord Vreeland had come upon them more quietly than was his habit, delighted at startling the ever-composed Fitzwilliam Darcy. It was a trick that he had used judiciously in Cambridge to crack the impenetrable mask the handsome young man used to fend off unwanted advances.

Darcy raised an eyebrow. "She encourages them, then?" he asked, sighing again at the disadvantages of marrying such an obvious beauty.

Hearing the pejorative nature in his cousin's voice, Fitzwilliam queried, "Did she encourage *you*, cousin? From across the dance floor while in the presence of her husband?"

Darcy was taken aback by the strident tone in Fitzwilliam defending the woman. "No," he conceded,

"I simply wonder, her being an unknown quantity of a girl."

"*You* have been away from town, Darcy, and have not spoken with her. You would like her, if you gave her the chance." Vreeland added.

Turning to admit their Cambridge comrade, Darcy said "I think not. A pretty face and pleasing… person, to be sure, but what sort of mind could she have? Raised in the wilds? Honestly, Fitzwilliam, you know me better than that, to be swayed by a woman only clever enough to catch a wealthy husband."

"Darcy? When did you return to town?" Rafael asked, a cold gleam in his eye. Darcy had the grace to blush before he looked at his friend, approaching from the right. Fitzwilliam looked at his cousin and Darcy noted a distinct look of displeasure spread over Richard's face as Rafael continued. "Allow me to introduce my wife." Rafael called to someone behind and to the left of Darcy who turned to find the woman who had taken his breath away, glaring at him. She had been speaking with Lady Madelyn Granby, daughter of the house. Elizabeth moved to her husband's side. "Elizabeth, this is Fitzwilliam Darcy, one of my *dearest* and oldest friends in this world. And you of course recall Colonel Fitzwilliam."

"Colonel! It is a pleasure to see you again. I so thoroughly enjoyed our discussion the other evening."

"Discussion? I call it a debate!" turning to his cousin, he said, "Darcy even you have not been able to challenge Donne's *Defense of Women's Inconsistency* as succinctly and as meaningfully as the Duchess." Darcy looked surprised.

"You are a student of poetry, your Grace?"

"Yes, sir. Even in the wilds of Hertfordshire, my home, we are rumored to have opened a book or two, and some of us are known to have even read them."

Darcy's color deepened as Elizabeth's brow arched, but her eyes held firm, filled with fire. Seeing him contrite, she relented at least momentarily. "However, Rafael tells me you have been in Ireland these many months and perhaps you have forgotten the love of literature that *all* English subjects have in their hearts. I hope you will join us one afternoon before we leave town and replenish your own taste for the bard and his brethren."

His look of confusion caused Rafael to laugh and explain, "Elizabeth has taken to Shelley and Miss Carter, and has held a weekly salon where the majority of our friends have returned to my… our home to partake of lively discussion of their latest work."

Assessing the woman before him anew Darcy realized his error and bowed. "I would be honored for an invitation to attend one of your salons, madam."

"I will bring you along, Darcy," Fitzwilliam added.

"You attend, cousin?"

"Indeed, I do. I would not miss one for the world. It is a marvel to witness, especially when her Grace plays chess with Coldwater."

"Coldwater? The London Chess Master?" Darcy was truly astonished.

"Yes, sir," Elizabeth added, mirth bubbling in her voice. "Mr. Coldwater would play, by correspondence, with my father. When Agatha introduced us, I continued the tradition, only playing in person.

"Singular." Darcy said before the pleasant conversation was interrupted by the acid tone of Caroline Bingley.

"Mr. Darcy! There you are." Seeing the Duke of Deronshire, she doubled her volume as she brashly took Darcy's arm in her hand. With him secure, she extended her other hand to Rafael. "Your Grace!"

Looking at first befuddled, Darcy stepped into the breach. Your Grace, may I introduce to you, Miss Bingley? She is sister to my friend, Charles Bingley."

"Ah! Then perhaps this is the evening I may actually meet this illusive friend of yours?" Rafael replied.

Elizabeth noticed the teasing her husband inflicted on the stoic Mr. Darcy, and that while not completely comfortable with it, he was able to bend a little. She quickly turned to face the newcomer taken aback by the avarice glaring in her eyes as the woman judged Elizabeth; her gaze resting on the diamonds and emeralds dangling from the neck of the new peer. Elizabeth could feel the envy festering.

"Miss Bingley," Darcy broke in the silence, "May I present her Grace, Elizabeth Gainsbridge, the Duchess of Deronshire? Your Grace? Miss Caroline Bingley."

"Charmed," Caroline oozed insincerely. As one of the minority of social scorpions who believed the Duke's marriage a disgrace, Miss Bingley made no pretense of hiding her disdain. "An honor to welcome you to London society. Tales of your rise from… obscurity… have enthralled London society. What a refreshing change it must be for you, my dear. Do call upon me, or my sister, Louisa… Louisa Hurst? If you ever need anything in your new station in life."

Aghast at her audacity, Elizabeth replied, "I shall keep your… generous… offer in mind, Miss Bingley." When Darcy was able to re-collect himself, he was stunned to see not the cold gaze that had met his own insult, but mirth dancing in Elizabeth's eyes. He watched as Rafael looked at her, sensing the silent communication between them, as his friend relaxed from concern for his bride, to pride and shared delight in her understanding the insignificance of Caroline's attempts to belittle. Darcy felt his heart contract in pain, wondering when, and if, such a woman could care for him.

"Yes, quite," Rafael said, not taking his eyes off Elizabeth. "If you will excuse us?" he asked his companions. They bowed and Elizabeth nodded her agreement. "Would you allow me another dance, my dear?"

Elizabeth giggled and smiling to her companions, left them on the arm of her husband. Fortunately for Darcy and Fitzwilliam, Charles Bingley arrived, and conversation turned toward matters of little interest to Caroline, forcing her to remain silent. Of the group, only Lord Vreeland paid her any mind, recognizing a social climber when he saw one, Vreeland was always on the look out for a new puppet.

While trying to restrain his gaze from the new Duchess, Darcy found his attention more often than not drifting to wherever it was that she stood in the great room. He noted the ease with which she conversed, and to his delight the artlessness of her laughter given freely and frequently to those happy enough to share her witty remarks. His preoccupation with the newlywed beauty was noted by many of the single and maternal women of the *ton*. One in particular could not help but notice when Darcy walked past her, oblivious to Miss Bingley's existence.

The only dark moment of the evening came when Darcy saw his friend sway and lean against a column. Within moments, Elizabeth was at his side, helping him to a secluded alcove. Wishing to be of assistance to his friend and closer, he admitted later to himself, to his friend's wife, Darcy followed them at a safe distance. What he saw shocked him, as Elizabeth coaxed Rafael to drink from a small vial she pulled from a pocket in her delectable gown. At first Rafael refused it, but Elizabeth pleaded until he relented, and taking the slender tube, drank it in one gulp. Satisfied he had imbibed what looked to be a repellant concoction, Elizabeth sat him in a chair and went through the archway so quickly Darcy had to step aside to avoid being caught spying on them. Returning with a glass of champagne, Elizabeth came up behind Darcy.

"Mr. Darcy, if you would be so kind as to call for our carriage? His Grace and I would ever be indebted to you."

Darcy nodded, surprised at the cold, calculated authority in her tone. Upon his return, noting Rafael's pallor and drained countenance, Darcy wondered what exactly was in the potion Elizabeth had given his friend. His suspicions increased by the recollection that Rafael had always been of strong constitution, besting both himself and his cousin if not in prowess, than in stamina. 'Rafael was always outwitting us, and yet I cannot believe that he would, could be outwitted by a... a woman. Even as bewitching a woman as Elizabeth.'

"Darcy," Rafael called struggling to stand.

"Your carriage awaits, Rafael," he said as he hurried to his friend's side.

"Thank you, Fitzwilliam," Rafael said, straightening himself.

He shook his head. While he said nothing, his eyes asked unspoken questions. Rafael held the arm of his friend, and gathering his strength to accompany Elizabeth rasped, "Come visit me soon, Darcy."

Darcy could only nod as the Duke and Duchess made their exit with quiet dignity amid the hubris of satin dolls and dandified men. Darcy stood thinking until he heard the strident tones of the approaching Miss Bingley, and he hurried into the card room where he remained until he could bring his evening to an end.

~

Darcy sent his card around to Wyndom House, residence of the Duke and Duchess, but was informed they were not accepting callers. It was two weeks before they were to meet again, at a dinner party at the home of the Earl of Matlock. When they were announced, Darcy's heart beat faster in the hope of seeing Elizabeth, and gaining the opportunity to engage her in conversation. The intervening social occasions had been full of talk of the mysterious beauty that now graced Wyndom House. The more scheming members of society were disparaging, while those of the progressive and intellectual circles praised her as a unique woman whose intellect matched her beauty. The one area where all could agree was the amount of control the new duchess seemed to exert over her husband. The more sagacious members of society accounted the withdrawal of the Duke to his being newly wed to such a vivacious woman, but Darcy was unconquered, and the varying opinions melded into an uncertain portrait of Rafael's new wife.

~

She wore a gown of iridescent blue, her eyes sparkling. A cross of sapphires hung precariously above the hollow between her breasts, her skin as clear and bright as her smile. Darcy was mesmerized. He felt himself in danger of betraying himself, and his friend. Darcy straightened to focus on the Duke who approached with outstretched arm.

"Darcy, you have been avoiding me!" he smirked.

Startled, Darcy looked to Elizabeth for an explanation. "No, Rafael, I have tried repeatedly. But was told you were not yet receiving visitors."

"Ah, well, we have been pre-occupied of late," the Duke replied as Elizabeth blushed. "We leave for Crystalglen within the month. You must come see us, and bring Georgiana. Agatha has been asking for her, and Elizabeth has expressed an interest in furthering the acquaintance."

"You have met ...?"

Both Rafael and Elizabeth smiled, but it was the Duke who replied, patiently. "Yes, Darcy. Your aunt and uncle brought her with them to our wedding, seeing as you were held captive in the wilds of Ireland for so long."

"Yes, however, if *you* had not married so hastily, I would have had ample time to return." As soon as the quasi-jest left his mouth, Darcy recognized his faux pas. "I did not mean... I apologize."

"You must forgive Fitzwilliam his prejudice, my dear," Rafael attempted to soothe the prickling he felt in Elizabeth. "Unless you deliberate for weeks on end, he does not consider one's judgment sound."

Rather than the icy glare Darcy expected, Elizabeth tilted her head and looked at him with a regard that pierced the mask so quickly put in place. He froze, dropping the façade, looking at her as would a young boy who had broken a window with a stray ball. "Only time will tell, Mr. Darcy," she said, her lips lifting in a smile, "Who is correct in their approach *and* their assumption."

"Very true, your Grace." He looked up into her confident smile. Expecting a confrontation, her smile confused him. Rafael's laughter shook him out of his reserve and the trio entered the general conversation until the footman announced the arrival of dinner.

~

Three days later, Georgiana and Fitzwilliam Darcy climbed the steps of Wyndom House and were welcomed by the Duke, Duchess and Dame Agatha. They spent a pleasant afternoon and Darcy was amazed at the ease with which Georgiana and Elizabeth conversed. Seeing his confusion, Elizabeth offered, "I have four sisters, Mr. Darcy. I am accustomed to female companionship. Your sister agreed to correspond with me and I have enjoyed her letters. And now," she took the younger woman's hand, "I am able to enjoy her company."

"Indeed? I was unaware..." he replied, deeply upset that his sister held a close connection to this enigmatic woman who so easily stormed his defenses.

"A woman must have her secrets, Mr. Darcy."

Darcy shot Elizabeth a look at which she turned her head to hide her mirth. He turned to look at his sister who sheepishly bent her head covering a smile.

"Darcy, may I steal you away from the delightful company of the ladies?" Rafael asked, rising from his chair.

"Of course." He too, rose, bowed to the women and followed his friend to the study. In the book lined room, Rafael went to the side board and poured a hefty glass of brandy. Turning to his friend he laughed at the shocked expression spread across the face of Fitzwilliam Darcy.

"Is it not a tad early for you, Rafael?"

The Duke barked a laugh.

"Rafe, what is it?" Darcy looked at the now empty glass in Rafael's hand. Dark thoughts crossed his mind and hesitating, he asked. "Is it Elizabeth?"

"My wife is not the source of my discontent," he spat. Rafael's fingers dragged across his lips, his eyelids closing, as if refusing to see a great unpleasantness. He then muttered to himself, "At least not directly, Darcy."

"Then what?"

"It is…" he turned and walked to the window. The Duke took a long drink, draining his glass. He stared out the window, looking out at the blossoms swaying in the trees across the street. He returned to the sideboard before continuing to speak. "Have you ever heard the story of how we met? Elizabeth and I? The full story?"

"No, I have only heard that you met in Vienna, returning smitten and courting this country miss."

"Yes, the country lass with *no fortune and few connections.* I swear if I hear that epitaph one more time, I will spit!"

"Rafael! Get a hold of yourself, man. I have never seen you so… agitated." Darcy was alongside the Duke, amazed at the color rising on his cheeks.

Taking a deep, calming breath, Rafael continued. "When in Vienna with Agatha..."

"That is another thing, Rafe, what were you doing in Vienna of all places! Do you not know what could have happened to you... *and* Dame Agatha if you were caught?" The Duke looked at his friend compassionately.

"I grant you that it was hazardous, however, we took... precautions to avoid... catching the interest of the authorities. And if I had not gone I would never have met Elizabeth..."

"And what, exactly was *she* doing there!?"

Knowing he could not reveal the diplomatic nature of Mr. Gardiner's mission, Rafael carefully guided the conversation back to his purpose. "She accompanied her uncle who took the necessary precautions, as well. What remains vital is that she is the woman who warmed my heart from the icy wasteland it had become. She challenged me, made me laugh, made me think, made me forget...." Rafael sighed. Rubbing his eyes he continued. "Darcy, Elizabeth is with child."

Darcy looked up from his thoughts to his friend. "Congratulations, Rafael!" While happy for his friend, Darcy was stunned by the swath of jealous pain running through his soul.

"Thank you, Darcy. I am... we are thrilled beyond measure. However, I feel..." his voice cracked, and Darcy looked away before the tears could fall from the eyes of his friend. Composing himself, Rafael returned the conversation to his first meeting Elizabeth. "When

I met Elizabeth, she was in Vienna with her uncle, Edward Gardiner. Do you know of him?"

"Gardiner? He owns the import business, down on Gracechurch Street, does he not?"

"Indeed."

"Yes, I believe my Uncle Fitzwilliam invests in one of his endeavors."

"Then he is a tad smarter than you. *My* Uncle Gardiner has a remarkable track record, and I believe I have uncovered his secret."

Darcy waited as long as he could well acquainted with the games his long-time friend preferred. "And that would be?"

"Elizabeth!"

Darcy began to speak, stopped then began again. "Elizabeth? You expect me to believe that *Elizabeth* is the secret to his success?"

"Elizabeth speaks five languages, fluently. She has demonstrated her uncommon sense in many matters during our brief time together. And Mr. Gardiner himself has all but admitted to me that it is his custom to run business prospects past Elizabeth for her opinion."

"Singular, indeed."

Rafael took in the dark eyes of his friend. He had resolved to ask this last favor of his friend, but now seeing Darcy so hostile to Elizabeth, he hesitated. "Darcy, I do wish you would surmount this suspicion you appear to have against her. Elizabeth carries my child, Darcy. My heir. It is one of my fondest wishes that my oldest, dearest friend and the love of my heart be friends."

Darcy was torn. He wanted to appease Rafael, but the agony of seeing Elizabeth happy with another ate at his contentment. He knew he must distance himself. Since seeing her nearly two months ago, her image had haunted him day and night. No woman of his acquaintance compared, and she belonged to another, to his dearest friend in the world. She made Rafael happy, happier than Darcy had ever seen him. And he coveted the liberty of taking her lips to his, of claiming her as his own. The battle lines were drawn, the battlefield, his heart.

"I will do my best, my friend."

"That is all I may ask," said Rafael after watching the torrent of emotion play upon his friend.

~ CHAPTER THREE ~

August, 1810
Crystalglen, Deronshire

The Darcy and Bingley carriages came to a stop at the main entrance to *Crystalglen.* Dame Agatha and Elizabeth waited on the steps. Darcy exited the coach, then turned to help his sister, Georgiana, out of their carriage. Charles Bingley bounded out of his coach followed by Stephen Hurst. Caroline Bingley emerged, momentarily dumbstruck by the splendor before her. When her eyes observed the obviously expecting Elizabeth, her expression soured. While never anticipating the attentions of the notoriously clever and witty, as well as fabulously wealthy Duke, it went against her snobbish disposition to accept that this country nobody, this Elizabeth Bennet, who absolutely '*no one* had ever heard of was now at the heart of the first circles of society.' She huffed as she climbed the first stair. 'Well, I for one will show her how far she had strayed from her natural sphere.'

The Bingleys ascended to their hostess.

"Welcome Georgiana, Mr. Darcy, Miss Bingley, Mrs. Hurst, Mr. Hurst, Mr. Bingley." Elizabeth greeted each with a warm smile, her hand settled on her expanded belly.

"My dear, how well you have *grown*... into your new position," cackled Caroline. "While no expert, I dare say you must have *anticipated* such splendor..." She looked accusatorily at Elizabeth then smirked at her sister, Louisa.

Stiffening at the implied insult, Dame Agatha stepped forward. "Not that it is any of your concern, Miss Bingley, however," she glanced at Elizabeth, who nodded her agreement, "We believe Elizabeth carries twins! They run in both our families." The matriarch gleamed like a school girl.

"Oh, Elizabeth! How magnificent!" cried Georgiana as she ran up to her friend and hugged her. "You must tell me all!"

Laughing Elizabeth said, "There is not much to tell. I am only grateful the wait is not twice as long."

With Dame Agatha on his arm, Darcy followed Elizabeth and Georgiana who were well ahead discussing future visits to *Crystalglen*, as Elizabeth would travel no more until the birth of her children, in December.

Taking his sister sternly in his arm, Bingley held her back. "Caroline, one more remark like that and you will find yourself on a coach to Aunt Adelaide in Scarborough."

"Brother!"

"Do you not see? We are here at Darcy's pleasure. Slighting our hostess, on her front steps no less, reflects poorly… not only on us, but on him! The Duke is one of Darcy's oldest friends. Whom do you think will fall out of favor? You, or the Duchess? Whom, I may add, has been nothing but gracious to you and myself, even though she has no obligation to be so, whatsoever."

Caroline walked in stunned silence, momentarily comprehending the precarious nature of her position. As the days progressed Caroline contained her intense irritation with the growing ease with which Elizabeth and Georgiana conversed. She also noted the way *her* Mr. Darcy looked at the Duchess and wondered what she could do to discredit the social upstart.

Caroline approached the breakfast table at her usual hour of half past ten. Standing at the portal to the now empty chamber, she surveyed the immaculately laid table. Greedily, her eyes devoured the fine china, the silver, glinting in the morning sun streaming through the sumptuous velvet drapes. Everything was impeccable, and it burned Caroline's fury into a rage. 'That all this glorious luxury is at the disposal of that, that chit…' and here she actually snorted, alerting the attention of Georgiana who was searching the halls for Elizabeth. The young woman hung back to escape Miss Bingley who now fondled the silver cutlery as someone,

Georgiana imagined, would caress a lover. Georgiana peeked around the corner of the doorframe as Caroline's eyes actually glazed over when she turned over the plate to read the china's mark. Georgiana nearly chortled aloud.

"It is not fair," Caroline stamped her foot as she whispered. "That… that woman has no right to all of this."

The dark look of hatred flushing Caroline's face frightened Georgiana, unused as she was to seeing such naked emotion. Her gasp alerted Caroline that she was not alone. Reacting to the intruder, Caroline quickly schooled her features into a veneer of fawning sincerity. Taking a deep breath, Georgiana advanced, unnerved when Caroline abandoned her aim of breakfast, to join Georgiana for a walk in the rose gardens.

∾

With each day the silent truce between the two women grew more and more strained until the tension became nearly unbearable, imposing greatly on the health of the Master and Mistress of Crystalglen. Elizabeth's stomach was in tumult more than the norm of a pregnant woman while the Duke seemed to fatigue easier than was his habit, his face gaunt, strained. He often excused himself from accompanying his guests due to a headache.

Finding Elizabeth alone in the solarium, Caroline positioned Louisa just at the doorway and began to speak. "I wonder at the Duke's embarrassment, Louisa."

"Embarrassment?" Louisa asked surprised at her sister's claim, and a bit annoyed she had disturbed her inspection of the blooming orchids laid out around her. "What on earth do you mean?"

"Why his obvious embarrassment over his choice of his wife, Louisa."

"Caroline," Louisa hissed, "Be quiet this instance. We are guests of their Graces. You will do well to remember that."

Caroline laughed. "I am not afraid of *her*, Louisa. She is a nobody, and once the Duke tires of her, she shall return to her proper sphere." Louisa looked at her sister, shock registering on her face. "Do not look so stupidly at me, my dear." Caroline looked beyond her stunned companion to the woman now sitting stiffly against the far wall. Caroline directed her sister away, so Louisa would not be distracted from playing her part in the charade. In doing so, Caroline did not see Elizabeth's companion, who had returned from ordering refreshments.

"It is spoken of in all the best houses," Caroline said with a forced laugh. "She is not one of *us* and will *never* be accepted as such. Poor deluded thing, believing she has friends in town. Although with the Duke's backing, she will never see the truth… until he sends her away."

Louisa pulled her arm away from her sister, staring at the malicious glint in Caroline's eye. "Caroline. That is a lie, and you know this. I have only heard praise for her Grace, in private as well as in public. You had best watch your tongue or you will find that you are the one who is alone with disapprobation hanging on your head." Louisa turned on her heel and stormed away. As she approached the door, she noted Elizabeth, who had managed to turn and look at the woman. Louisa was horrified, but Elizabeth just smiled weakly at her and nodded her head. Executing a shallow curtsey, Louisa left, her cheeks colored with shame.

"Elizabeth," Agatha called loudly, the force of anger in her words. "I have ordered tea and scones." Agatha looked directly and unflinchingly at Caroline, "Ah, Miss Bingley, I had not seen you there. Have you been here long?" Agatha advanced, her glare freezing Caroline where she stood. Attempting to charm her way out of her embarrassment, Caroline tried to smile but failed miserably, her lips drawn into a tight grimace.

Moving to join the matriarch of society, Caroline replied, "But a moment, Dame Agatha." Seeing the frosty glare in the older woman's eyes, Caroline recoiled and stopped moving to join her hostess.

Agatha continued, never letting her eyes release her guest. "The post has come, and I just received a letter from Lady Montesford." She lifted the letter still in her hands. "My friend mentions your latest attempt to gain access to Almack's. Pity that." She looked at her niece. "If only you had asked Elizabeth for help. Not only was *her* application accepted, but she has become such a favorite of Lady Balfore. Such a shame... Perhaps next year." Agatha stopped as if in thought. "But then you would still require two sponsors, would you not? Perhaps Lady McNichols would consider sponsoring you? Oh, but then there was that terrible faux pas, was there not?. Something about her daughter, Alicia?" Agatha advanced. "Lady McNichols is a dear friend, but I dare say she is not apt to forget such a slight as calling her daughter plain and a twittering chit, now is there?" Agatha had cornered Caroline against the window panes, pinning her there with a glance holding her without mercy. "Funny thing, families... especially old families... tenaciously loyal... and we do tend to band together against the onslaught battering at the door. So democratic in their demands... do you not agree?"

Elizabeth had, by now, struggled to rise from her chair, and waddled over to the women. "Agatha?"

Agatha swung her head, looking for any signs of distress on Elizabeth's face. "Yes, my dear?"

"I was hoping you would walk with me. I find myself in need of air." Elizabeth advanced with as much dignity as an extremely pregnant woman could muster. Her face was radiant and her eyes danced in delight. She looked at the stricken face of Miss Bingley before turning her most brilliant smile to Agatha.

Taking one last look at Caroline, her eyes slashing the interloper, Agatha moved toward Elizabeth and said, "Of course."

The two left the solarium for a stroll through the gardens. Caroline turned to slump against the glass, grateful for the condensation that cooled her brow. Her breathing was hard to control, as she relived the humiliation of being turned away, yet again from gaining acceptance at Almack's. Her connections and her fortune were both found lacking. She had not heeded the warning of her brother, so confident was she in her association with the Darcys and her *friends* from school. But they had proved to be feckless, abandoning her when word circulated of her ill-timed set down of Alicia McNichols' attempt to engage Mr. Darcy in conversation.

When the serving girl entered with the tea, she found the solarium abandoned.

∾

A week after the Darcy's party departed, Jane Bennet came to her sister. One month later, Madelyn Gardiner arrived with her three children to help her favorite niece prepare for her confinement. Mrs. Bennet was unable to attend, as Mr. Bennet had fallen from his horse. While rendered unconscious for three days, the doctors were hopeful he would make a full recovery. Constant communication was maintained between Longbourn the Bennets estate and Crystalglen, easing the guilt felt by both daughters who were told to banish thoughts of traveling home.

Early November brought the return of the Darcys. As promised, Georgiana was to remain with the Gainsbridges until Elizabeth delivered of her children. She would be kept away from the birthing chamber but was more than willing to attend Elizabeth and keep her spirits away from the dark thoughts and fears that often dog expectant women.

~

A gentle knock awakened Madelyn Gardiner. "Enter," she called, rising to find a candle in the dark room.

"Madam?" Maria called out, her voice barely above a whisper.

Recognizing her niece's abigail, Madelyn asked, "Maria, is Elizabeth well?"

"Oh, Ma'am, her Grace is in a bad way."

Madelyn's hand rose to her face. "She is in pain?" She was out of bed, hunting for her robe.

"Only in her heart, ma'am."

This stopped Madelyn who turned toward the girl, assessing what had just been said. Maria lowered her eyes, bending to light Madelyn's candle with her own. When the girl looked up again, she said, "She fears for the unborn."

"Ah, I am ready. Bring me to her."

Quickly the women returned to the Master's bedchamber. As they entered they heard Elizabeth's sobs and the low murmuring of her husband trying to soothe her.

"Elizabeth?" her aunt called gently, as she tentatively approached the bed. Rafael looked up, startled at her presence. Both he and Madelyn Gardiner looked accusingly at Maria who bent her head, avoiding their questioning eyes.

Rafael returned his focus to Elizabeth as a fresh sob escaped her lips. "Hush, my love, all will be well. Your aunt is here."

Elizabeth looked up, tears staining her cheeks and she sniffled back a gasp.

"Elizabeth! Child, what is it?" asked the older woman now sitting on the side of the bed. Gently she stroked Elizabeth's cheek, wiping away the moisture.

"Oh, Aunt, I am afraid," she whispered.

"Of course you are, my dear. Every woman has fear when their time draws near."

"Were you afraid, aunt?" asked Rafael hoping she would help calm his bride.

"Oh, yes. At each and every birth." She held Elizabeth's hand, covering it with the other. "It is a fear born of love," both Elizabeth and Rafael looked at her. "Oh yes, the love we have for our yet unborn children. Will they be well? Will I be a good mother? As good as they deserve?" Seeing Elizabeth relax, Madelyn decided to broach the crux of the matter that weighs on every expectant mother. With a deep breath and a silent prayer, she continued. "Will I survive to take care of my children?" Her niece and nephew both gasped. Madelyn looked directly at her niece. "Elizabeth, every woman must face these fears. You must believe," she squeezed her niece's hand tightly. "You will be well, my dear. You *must* believe this, with all your heart. The doctors are well pleased with you and the way you are progressing. You must have faith."

"It is not easy, aunt!"

"I know, Lizzy, I know. That is why it is crucial to have those who love you here for you," she gently pushed back a fallen curl. "To bolster your spirit when it flags. We are here, my dear, to carry you when you are too tired. That is what family is for, to love and aid you."

"Oh, aunt," Elizabeth embraced her aunt, releasing more tears.

"Let it out, dearest, let this fear fall from your heart, and you will see in the morning, your strength returns." They remained thus for nearly half-an-hour, until Madelyn transferred her sleeping niece back into the arms of her grateful husband.

"Thank you, Aunt," he whispered once Elizabeth was safely tucked in his embrace.

"'Tis what my own aunt once did for me, Rafael. Truly, it is what family does for each other."

With a quick touch to his arm, Madelyn returned to her chamber, and fell to her knees in a silent petition for the protection and wellbeing of her favorite niece.

~

Darcy returned to Pemberley his heart heavy with the feelings he could not control. 'She is,' he thought morosely. 'Everything I could ever want, except that she is the wife of my best friend.' Again he turned his head as if he could turn her out of his thoughts. He took up his quill trying to complete another piece of correspondence.

~

Elizabeth's fears continued to wax and wane as her time drew to a close. The women and Rafael kept her as diverted as possible with Madelyn and Agatha attending her on the dark nights of her soul.

Her daily constitutional became a longer and more significant event, as her extended belly offset her innate balance and stamina. She walked, accompanied by her husband, or one of her family and a footman who could run off in search of aid, if needed. At first she teased them about their solicitousness, but as her belly grew exponentially, she was grateful to be so well protected.

One of the concerns weighing Elizabeth's heart was the frequency she noted Rafael needing his tonic. Meersham had become quite proficient at mixing the components together, and on one occasion Elizabeth observed his preparations. Noting the increased strength she queried, "Is it truly necessary, Meersham?"

Startled, the faithful valet jumped and turned around. About to make a neutral reply he stopped, looking at his mistress. There, before him stood an enormously pregnant woman, with a look of pure horror in her eyes. She knew the significance of the new dose. There was no use in hiding the truth from her. He nodded.

"How long has His Grace needed this new formulation?"

"A week, or two, madam."

"How much... stronger?"

"By half, your Grace."

Elizabeth nodded. "You will tell me if..." she closed her eyes, only to open them quickly. "When... he requires more?" she asked and Meersham noticed the tears collecting in the corners of her beautiful eyes, eyes that danced and welcomed, and brought life, joy and comfort to a dying man. "Of course, madam."

Elizabeth nodded then left the room. Silently, Meersham bowed his head, his hands grasping the work counter for support. 'Indeed, how shall we all ever survive?' he asked himself, not for the first time.

After a lengthy but relatively safe labor, Rafael William Gainsbridge and Ian Thomas Gainsbridge were born, one month early, on November 25th, in the hours of three and then four in the afternoon. Mother and children recovered relatively quickly from the trauma of birth. Rafael, breaking all precedent had remained with his wife throughout her labor, washing her brow, holding her hand and whispering soft words of comfort, skills taught to him by his loving wife.

January, 1811
Pemberley, Derbyshire

Darcy read the express sent by his sister informing him of her early return to London.

"Brother,

Due to unforeseen circumstances, the Gainsbridges and I shall return to London as soon as we may. I, of course, will return with them, remaining at Wyndom House until your arrive in London. While I have enjoyed my time with Dame Agatha, Elizabeth, Rafael and the twins, I would ask you retrieve me as soon as possible, as to unburden them in their time of need. Oh, Brother, it is enough to break one's heart, to witness such devotion and heartbreak in the same moment. But I remain strong, and seek comfort with Dame Agatha, and the children. They grow right before my eyes. I try to keep away from Elizabeth as she must carry this burden alone.

Until we meet again, I remain your devoted sister,

GD"

Provisions were made to leave Pemberley at first light. The Gainsbridge party would already be in London. Darcy wondered at the magnitude of distress that would force them to leave the comfort of Crystalglen, with infants barely two months old. 'Devotion and heartbreak!' he held the parchment's edge to his lips, running it over their smooth fullness. 'Could it be Elizabeth? Now that the heir is provided, does she make some new demand?' Thoughts of Elizabeth breaking her marriage vows darkened Darcy's eyes. 'She would be free, but inaccessible to me for such betrayal. Rafe is my oldest friend.' Such was the state of his thoughts during the two day carriage ride. The heat of envisioning Elizabeth engaged in an illicit rendezvous countered the late January cold.

~

Darcy traveled to Wyndom House as quickly as possible. He rode Xander the few blocks to Belgravia Square and was admitted to the Master's study. As he stood beside the blazing fire, Darcy's thoughts darkened recalling the urgency of his summons. His mind formulated plans for removing the wayward Duchess, thinking of suitable estates far from the glare of London. Estates coincidently, easily accessible from Derbyshire. The sound of the door opening drew him back to the present. He turned and nearly swooned as his friend, thin, grey and leaning heavily on a cane, made his way slowly to the fire.

"Darcy! Thank you for coming on such a bitter night as this." Darcy was unable to speak. Rafael's eyes raked over the vibrant form of his boyhood friend. "Quite a sight, I imagine, eh? Not what you expected..." Rafael wearily made his way to the fire. "Pour me a brandy, would you, my friend?"

"Of course," Darcy said, relieved for something to give him distance and the chance to gain some perspective. He quickly poured a snifter for himself as well as his host. He walked over to the fire and sat himself opposite the Duke. Rafael eagerly took the beverage and gulped it down. As the amber liquid restored him, he sighed, smiled and leaned back in his chair. "Do not tell Elizabeth of my indulgence. There will be hell to pay soon enough."

"Rafe, what is it? What has she done?"

"She? What...? Do you... you think *Elizabeth* is responsible for... for my condition?" he asked incredulously.

Darcy, keeping his eyes on his friend, replied, "I do," he hesitated. "I saw the potion she gave you at the Granby ball..."

"Potion? My wife is no witch, Darcy!" his responding laugh was dark.

"No? She bewitched..." Darcy sprang from his chair to collect himself as he paced the room, "*You* out of your senses! Agreeing to a such a precipitous marriage." He scoffed trying to cover his near revelation. "Now she seeks to hasten your demise through poison. She secludes you at the estate so we, your friends, cannot assist you... now that I am here I will remove Georgiana ... and assist in plans to cast..."

"Stop! Darcy, before you embarrass yourself further." Darcy stopped short and Rafael continued. "Darcy, sit." He waited until his friend complied. "Darcy." Rafael looked to his friend, and his tone softened "William. I suffer with a cancer... in my belly. It is what brought me to Vienna, where Elizabeth and I met. Dr. Grimwald... Agatha and I sought treatment from

Dr. Frankelstone. What you think you saw Elizabeth give me was *his* vile concoction, not some poison."

"Cancer?" Darcy was stunned. He sat motionless, the word reverberating in his head.

While the truth of his condition filtered through his friend's defenses, Rafael watched till finally he said, gravely, "Yes."

Darcy turned away. His mind still numb, he asked, "For how long?"

"I have known for almost five years. It is only in the last two that the pain," he hesitated, "has become a nuisance."

Silence descended upon the two men who had accompanied each other throughout their lives. First marriage and now death threatened to separate their fates. "Darcy… I…" here the Duke leaned forward. "It is my dearest wish that *you* will take care of my sons… and Elizabeth."

"I… of course I will guide your sons, Rafe. But El… she…"

Rafael looked his closest friend in the eye. "I will say this only once, Fitzwilliam. I have known you since we were still with leading strings. I… we entered society together. I have never seen you react to a woman the way you have to Elizabeth."

"Rafael! I never…!"

The Duke held up his hand to still his agitated friend. "I know this, William. I accuse you of nothing. Please, let me continue." Darcy looked away. "I ask that you take on Elizabeth as well." He inhaled deeply. "I ask that you promise to marry Elizabeth once I am... gone."

"Rafael, you cannot be serious." Darcy experienced true shock.

"But I am, Darcy. Think of it. Elizabeth is a beautiful woman, and soon, she will be a very beautiful, very wealthy widow."

Looking sharply at his friend, Darcy finally acknowledged the truth of his statement and Elizabeth's soon-to-be condition. "I spoke without thinking. Did she know of your... condition before you married?"

"Of course she knew before we married! I would not saddle her..."

"With your fortune!" Darcy's anger rose unexpectedly.

"With my illness!" Darcy was silenced. Rafael continued. "With the retching, the soiling my clothes, the hours of agony. No. I would not do that to anyone, let alone the woman I love! Elizabeth knew before we wed, but after I proposed... what my condition had become. I am a selfish creature. I wanted, needed to know... that if healthy, she would accept me. Then, I gave her the opportunity to back away from her promise. Yet she remains at my side, night and day, always here to ease my pain. You have no idea the release that comes from a pair of compassionate eyes in the face of a beautiful, loving woman." Rafael held out his snifter for his friend to refill. "And if you do not think it tears me up inside to know it will not be *me* growing old with that woman, than you know nothing at all."

It took nearly five minutes before Rafael could master his emotions to speak. "This is my final request, my friend. My last favor…"

"Surely not…"

"It may well be, Darcy. It is my greatest wish that *you* look after my children… and it is my fondest… desire… that you *marry* Elizabeth."

~ CHAPTER FOUR ~

April, 1811
Crystalglen, Deronshire

Three months after his conversation with Fitzwilliam Darcy, Rafael Gainsbridge, the Duke of Deronshire, was dead. His last days were spent with loved ones gathered round. Elizabeth had brought the boys into the darkened room, allowing them to snuggle as she placed his arms around them, holding them tight to his chest. His sunken cheeks nuzzled their downy heads and he kissed them repeatedly, as if endowing them with enough kisses to last their lifetimes. Elizabeth refused to leave his side, spooning broth and water through his parched lips. She wiped his brow and even hours after he slipped into unconsciousness, she told him of her love, that she was there and he would be in her heart forever.

When Agatha came to sit with Rafael, Elizabeth remained, curled alongside her husband, his rasping breath her only assurance he was still there.

"Agatha?" she asked, weary from the weight of the last twenty-four hours.

"Yes, my dear?" replied the older woman.

"You will wake me… you *will* wake me if… if…"

"Yes, Elizabeth. I will."

Elizabeth nodded their understanding as she snuggled along beside him. Her children rested in their cots nearby, and as Elizabeth felt her heavy lids close, she smiled at the still warm arm that embraced her, and at the movement of her hand, resting lightly on her husband's chest. She turned his face toward her and kissed his lips. When Elizabeth woke hours later, Rafael was physically there, but not responding. Shocked, Elizabeth jolted up, looking in horror between Rafael and Agatha who had moved to calm her anxious niece.

"Is he?" Elizabeth asked. Agatha came and sat beside her on the bed.

"No, child, he rests only." Agatha responded, as she gently pushed a curl from Elizabeth's forehead.

Straightening, Elizabeth quickly kissed her husband before leaving to refresh herself. When she returned, Agatha said, "I have ordered coffee." She turned to look towards the cots. "The boys slept through the night."

"You must be ready for a rest, are you not?" Elizabeth asked.

Looking at the rail thin man lying in his bedclothes, she replied, "No, I believe I shall sit with you a bit longer." Looking Agatha in the eye, Elizabeth understood that Rafael was lost to them, only his breath remained, his essence earthbound no more. She crumpled against the bed post, tears streaming down her face, as she clung to the wooden rail. Trying to reign in her emotions, she called out, her voice broken, "I love you Rafael. I love you. But… but if it is your time… then go..."

Elizabeth allowed Agatha to lead her to a chair, which she dragged to the side of the bed. She took Rafael's hand, stroking it gently as she whispered, "You are so loved, my darling. If it is your time, let go." Her tears were uncontainable, as she buried her face on his hand, repeating, "Rafael, my love, you are mine forever. I love you, but you may go. Remember me."

Rafael's mouth closed, his lungs stilled, Elizabeth raised her head sharply. All eyes – Elizabeth, Agatha, Dr. Grimwald, Meersham, and Maria – all fastened on the still body until he opened his mouth again, releasing the air from his lungs into the room. Their collective release filled the silence as they each took a chair, moving closer to the bed to keep vigil for their lover, friend, nephew, patient and employer. Silently they recalled the way his eyes smiled, his lips curling in delight, or a remark he made that had caught them unaware. They remained with him until his end, and he breathed no more.

~

Elizabeth was distraught, worn from months of ceaseless care bestowed on her beloved husband, coupled with the demands of mothering twins. As much as Agatha loved her nephew, she believed in the living. She watched with grave concern as her niece lost weight, became listless. With the single mindedness she was famous for, Agatha removed the grieving family to their summer estate, Brookhaven, near Ramsgate, feeling that the healing beauty of nature would revive Elizabeth, pulling her back to life.

As the air warmed, the women walked along the seaside, allowing the air, beauty and constancy of the sea to soothe their souls. The boys grew, thriving on the unconditional love given by their mother and great aunt. Elizabeth cherished her children who gave her hope, and a reason to smile. She had loved her husband, but it was the numbing strain of tending him during his last weeks that remained with her. When she looked at her children, she saw their eyes full of life and joy and slowly, with time, she let go her grief and pain, grasping on to their love and joy of living.

On one of their walks along the shore, Agatha and Elizabeth noticed a familiar figure a ways ahead.

"Georgiana!" Elizabeth called out, ignoring propriety. The young woman turned and registering their identities, hurried toward them. Panting to catch her breath, she gasped, "Elizabeth! Dame Agatha! How glorious to see you!" Georgiana embraced Elizabeth then Agatha.

"What brings you here to Ramsgate?" the girl asked.

"We are ensconced at Brookhaven." Agatha looked over to her niece. "Elizabeth wished for some sea air, and here we are," replied the older woman. "I may ask the same of you, my dear."

"Fitzwilliam removed me from school and I, with my companion," here she pointed back along the promenade, "Mrs. Younge, have taken a house for the next two months… on Blascomb Street."

Elizabeth smiled, delighted to see her young friend. "You are well?"

"Oh, yes!" Georgiana blushed and looking down the way at the approaching figure of a man, she smiled. Elizabeth and Agatha followed her gaze before sharing knowing looks. Agatha looked toward Mrs. Younge, noting that the companion kept more than a polite distance. "And the boys? How are they? They must be enormous by now." The older women nodded and they all burst into laughter.

"They are indeed, my dear," said Elizabeth, and taking Georgiana's hand they began walking. "You must promise to come and visit, and see for yourself. I dare say they could use some new stimulation. It has been only Agatha, myself and their nurse since…" Elizabeth looked away, out to sea. Georgiana and Agatha exchanged concerned glances between them. Each took one of Elizabeth's arms, giving her a squeeze as they walked. Elizabeth smiled weakly and continued, "Please, say you will come, Georgiana. I would so enjoy your company. Not that Agatha hasn't been wonderful, for she has." Agatha laughed.

George Wickham approached and bowed to the women. Elizabeth startled when she heard the name, recalling her late husband's opinion when they had seen him in the park, prior to leaving for Crystalglen. *"A more dissolute reprobate I shall not wish to imagine, my dear. When you see George Wickham come to town, lock up your women and your valuables, in that order."*

Elizabeth appraised the gentleman before her, 'He looks harmless.' But then Elizabeth noticed his expression when introduced, feeling his eyes rake over her black clad form.

Agatha and Elizabeth made their farewells soon after, and as they passed the woman Georgiana had indicated was her companion, Agatha spoke. "You are Mrs. Younge, are you not?" The woman nodded. "Then you had best do your job and chaperone your *young* charge who now walks with Mr. Wickham, *alone*."

The woman blushed and walked closer to Georgiana looking back to see both Elizabeth and Agatha watching with unfaltering attention.

~

A week later, Elizabeth received an express from Longbourn with the distressing news that Mr. Bennet had taken ill. Having never fully recovered from his fall months prior, the power of speech was lost to him. Jane pleaded for Elizabeth's return to placate her mother, whose incessant lamentations were distressing all. Wishing to make all possible haste, Elizabeth sent word to Georgiana, requesting her help in caring for the twins. Georgiana readily agreed to the request.

The two weeks since Elizabeth's departure passed quickly for Georgiana and Agatha, attending the nearly six month old twins. As they watched the boys play on a blanket in the shade, Georgiana expressed her desire for a family of her own.

"But you are still prodigiously young, child! Surely you wish to taste a bit more of life before settling down!" Agatha exclaimed.

"Elizabeth was barely older than I when she met Rafe, Dame Agatha."

Agatha looked at Georgiana, the vision of George Wickham's covetous eye appraising both Georgiana and Elizabeth coming unbidden to her. "Yes, she was," the septuagenarian replied. "Yet she had travelled extensively and had at least tasted of the world. And *their* circumstances were different, as you know."

Georgiana thought of the rapidity of the Gainsbridge's courtship. Agatha continued. "Even, with all their *urgency*, all the formalities of a *proper* courtship were followed." Georgiana looked up at this. "Rafael felt Elizabeth deserved this... being courted. He, a duke, went to Mr. Bennet, a country gentleman, for his consent. When his feelings grew to where he wished to marry Elizabeth, he was honest with her, *and* her family. Georgiana, he told them of his illness, that his end was near, and that it would be beastly. He honored her intelligence and sensibility by risking her disapprobation. It was the only way for them both to be sure of their feelings for each other, and for him to enter the marriage with a clear conscience."

Throughout Agatha's discourse, Georgiana thought about Wickham. At the time he had first suggested eloping, she found it thrilling, daring and extremely romantic. But now, sitting with Agatha, she acknowledged another, darker shade to his request.

"Agatha? Did Rafael ever mention George Wickham?" she asked, hesitation in her voice.

Agatha thought carefully before speaking. "Yes, my dear, he did. Why do you ask?"

"It is just... simply..." and before she could think twice upon it, the entire story of her entanglement with George Wickham tumbled from her mouth. When done, Georgiana pledged Agatha to secrecy after promising to remain with either Agatha or Elizabeth, until Fitzwilliam could come and collect her. In return, Agatha extracted the additional pledge of telling Fitzwilliam of Wickham's advances.

When George Wickham arrived at Brookhaven, a letter awaited expressing the nature of Georgiana's obligation to the Gainsbridge children, and her desire to wait another month before proceeding. 'At least she is not completely refusing to see me,' he thought. 'Perhaps I may yet salvage something of this scheme.' Mounting his horse his mind strayed to the ways the widow Younge could help pass the time, a lecherous smile stretching his lips. With a last look at the well tended drive just out of reach behind the locked gate, he said, "Yes, Georgiana, keep your love and your money and give it to those little boys. This *man* will seek his solace with a real woman." Focusing on his impatient horse he said, "But I shall return. On *that* you may rely."

~

Elizabeth's return was a cause for great celebration at Brookhaven. The boys were calmer and happier in their mother's presence, and Georgiana knew she could trust Elizabeth to help sort through her feelings for George Wickham.

She found Elizabeth in the solarium overlooking the surf pounding in the distance. A light rain trickled down the panes of glass, the sky overhung in grey. The room was the brightest in the house, and Georgiana was not surprised to find her friend clinging to what light remained. "Elizabeth, a moment of your time?"

Turning to look at her companion, Elizabeth replied, "Of course, Georgiana." The girl approached tentatively. "Does something press upon you?" Expecting a pleasant reply, Elizabeth was shocked at the forlorn expression of her friend. Instantly, she was at the young girl's side. "My dear, what troubles you?"

"Elizabeth, how did you know you were in love?"

By the look on Elizabeth's face, this was not the question she had anticipated. "Love? Are you in love, my dear?"

Georgiana pulled away. "I no longer know." Bursting into sobs she said. "I believed it to be so, but now... I am no longer sure."

"With whom are you in love, dearest?" Elizabeth asked gently, her fingers teasing the hair out of Georgiana's eyes.

"George Wickham," was all the girl could whisper.

"Wickham? No!" Georgiana looked up, shocked by the vehemence of Elizabeth's reply. Looking around, Elizabeth escorted them both to a chaise by the wall of glass. When they had settled, Elizabeth began. "Once, before the twins were born, when Rafael and I were still in town, he returned home one evening, terribly upset." Georgiana sniffled. "He had encountered George Wickham, inebriated, and boasting of former conquests. One in particular, was the daughter of a Gainsbridge tenant. Rafael tempered the description, but suffice it to say, Wickham had extolled her *charms* rather freely to his audience. Rafael was distraught. The girl had died delivering Wickham's child. He was terribly upset, as Wickham's boasts had brought up the horrific details of the girl's last hours. Rafael's mother had been called in to assist as much as possible. From what he said, the Duchess was compassionate beyond measure." Georgiana nodded. "Rafael remembered all those years later her returning to Crystalglen, her dress soaked in the blood of the innocent."

Both women sat in silence. Georgiana's gaze remained fixed on her hands. Elizabeth trained her eyes on the girl. Finally, Elizabeth again spoke gently.

"I believe... that anyone who is that callous towards the fate of one he has endangered... is not one to trust, especially with something as tender and precious as your heart."

Georgiana only nodded. After what felt like hours, Georgiana whispered, "Thank you, Elizabeth. You have shown me a side of Wickham I had not known." The young woman looked up, looking older, sadder, and perhaps a bit wiser.

"Of course... you could not have known. These things are not spoken of."

"Perhaps they should be." There was steel in Georgiana's voice and in her eyes. "Then women would not be so susceptible to such brutes."

Elizabeth slipped her arm around Georgiana, and hugged her to her side. "Perhaps, my friend. But now we know, and shall no longer fall prey to one such as he." Georgiana turned away. "Oh my dear," Elizabeth assessed the situation. "He has touched your heart, already?"

"Yes... no. I am no longer certain. I thought so, but now, hearing of his actions, I shudder to think how false and manipulative his words to me have been."

"What transpired between you, Georgiana? Will you trust me?"

"Yes, Elizabeth. I will." Georgiana took a deep breath and began. "When Mrs. Younge and I arrived here in Ramsgate, we found Geor... Mr. Wickham. He recalled so many pleasant times... from before... from before my father's death." The young woman hesitated before adding, softly. "Mrs. Younge seemed to encourage his attentions." Elizabeth's spine tingled at this. "We would encounter him on the promenade, the bookstore, or the concert hall. He even accompanied us to services!"

"Oh, dear!" Elizabeth said, surprised. "Georgiana, you said that your companion, Mrs. Younge encouraged his attention to you?" There was a hint of alarm in her voice.

"Yes, so it seemed."

"If I may be so bold to ask, how?"

Georgiana thought for a moment. "She… would… speak so well of him when he came upon us. Saying, 'what a fine gentleman,' and 'what a treasure to find an old, trusted friend,' things of that sort. And she would let us walk together, while she kept her pace back a step or two."

"I see." Elizabeth changed her train of thought. "Georgiana, have you told your brother of this?"

The girl ducked her head and then shook it. "No, not yet."

"I suggest you do." Georgiana looked up. Elizabeth took pity on the look of alarm on the girl's face. She chuckled. "It will not be *that* bad." When the fear did not abate, Elizabeth offered, "Would you wish me to… write to him?"

"Oh, would you, Elizabeth? Please?" Her reply was immediate.

Her lower lip was held between her teeth, but her eyes held compassion. "Yes, if it will ease your mind."

"Oh, thank you, Elizabeth. You are magnificent!"

'Indeed,' the older woman thought, wondering what she had gotten herself in to.

When the silence caught her attention, Elizabeth looked to her companion and Georgiana crumbled.

"He said he loved me, Elizabeth, and I so desperately wanted to be loved!"

"Oh, Georgiana!" Elizabeth embraced the young woman as she unleashed the tears of her heart. Gently rocking the girl in her arms, she smoothed her golden curls. "There, there. Hush." She held her tightly. "All is well, Georgi, all is well, as long as we live and breathe, my dear. We all long for love, Georgiana. For our own shining heart, to have and to hold." Elizabeth held Georgiana until the sobs became whimpers and finally she was able to pull back, her eyes red and puffy, but with a calmness that had been missing earlier.

When Wickham returned to Brookhaven two weeks later, he found the doors barred, with word that Miss Darcy, the Duchess and her family had departed. There was nothing else, no mention of regard. Wickham's jaw clenched as he glared at the gatekeeper. Assessing the tall fence and the burly footmen who accompanied the elderly man, Wickham abandoned his notion of storming the gates in an overt, dramatic gesture designed to sway the romantic sensibilities of the young, impressionable heiress. Instinctively he recognized that united with the Duchess and Dame Agatha, Georgiana was well beyond his reach. He may be able to dupe the ingénue, but the widow and Dowager would not be so easily beguiled.

"Until another day then, eh?" he swaggered up to his horse. There was that delectable Miss King whose acquaintance he had recently made in Bath. "Miss Darcy is not the only fruit ripe for the plucking."

It was with trepidation that Darcy looked upon Crystalglen. He was glad to reunite with his sister after her experience with Wickham. The express from Elizabeth had sent him in a wild fury and Darcy took measures to have Wickham watched, carefully. As the carriage proceeded down the drive, Darcy recalled the many times he had made this journey in the past visiting Rafael while on break from school, or on family visits. 'Now, I know not what I shall find. Strangers in familiar halls.' "Elizabeth!" His heart exclaimed and he drew a deep breath. "Elizabeth and her sons rather than Rafael and his parents."

Taking the parchment from his coat pocket, he reread the letter in her hand.

Dear Mr. Darcy,

I write on behalf of your sister, Georgiana. Fear not, she is well, only a recent encounter with an old friend of yours, Mr. George Wickham, has left her heart, unsettled.

Based upon what Rafael had revealed of his character, Agatha and I have taken Georgiana into our home, preventing any further encounter with said gentleman. I must inform you that based on direct observation, along with what Georgiana has recounted, that Mrs. Younge worked to advance Mr. Wickham's cause.

Georgiana is well, as well as may be expected, and is heartily embarrassed by recent events. She, and her reputation remain unblemished, and I implore you to consider her tender heart and age when next you meet.

We await your arrival at Crystalglen at your earliest convenience. Our departure is set for tomorrow. Georgiana has been a great joy and is always welcome here.

Sincerely,
Elizabeth Gainsbridge,
Duchess of Deronshire

'Elizabeth!' he again exhaled, her image filling his mind. He had not seen her since the funeral nearly four months before. Even in grief Elizabeth outshone all who had gathered and he wondered how he would contain the overpowering feelings that had only grown towards this enigma of a woman.

~ CHAPTER FIVE ~

June, 1811
Crystalglen, Deronshire

Agatha and Georgiana were at the door to greet Darcy, explaining that Elizabeth was occupied in the nursery, settling her sons into their nap. They were teething and peevish. In fact, all three women had spent the morning, their attention focused on the young gentlemen, attempting to ease their fussiness away. Her absence gave him time to acclimate being at Crystalglen under its new management, and prepare himself to face her. He was shown to his room, and after a quick bath, went in search of her.

Despite all he had heard from Rafael before his death, the disparaging remarks of Miss Bingley and the news he received in Georgiana's letters, nothing compared to the imagery his dreams and fancy had created. Rarely had a day gone by when he was not undone by a vision of her beauty. And nightly, his dreams were full of her, as he more than willingly fulfilled his friend's parting wish in taking Elizabeth to his marital bed.

Her laughter led him to the Master's study. It amused him that she would take over Rafael's personal domain. As Rigels opened the door, Darcy was surprised at the scene awaiting him. There stood Elizabeth, with six month old Rafael snuggled in her arms. His alert gaze followed his mother's hand as she pointed to a portrait of Rafael hanging above the mantle.

"And this, my little man, is your father. This is his study. His room. This is where he took care of us and so many others. And with time, and a bit of guidance," here she wiggled her nose to the child's. "You will learn to do the same. Your Pappa," her voice caught in grief, she took a deep breath before continuing, her tone as soft as a kiss. "Was a wonderful man, my love. His duty was no burden." Emotion cracked her voice. "And we shall ensure the same for you."

Darcy stood, her words conjuring Rafael's last request that he, Darcy, look after the family Rafael was leaving behind. He had spent the last four months selfishly thinking only of Elizabeth: the unsuitability of her birth, her lack of connections, how his lust for her burned against the guilt he still harbored at desiring the wife of his closest friend. And now, she stood before him, free, his for the taking. Rafael's plea to care for his family waged against the fire in his blood. Desire and duty combined to squash the whisper of caution that echoed through his mind. 'She *will* welcome me!' his lust urged him onward. 'I have Rafe's blessing.' His need for her to smile for him alone, for the sparkle of her eyes to shine for him, to feel the softness of her skin against his shut the door on rational thought and he nodded to Rigels to announce him.

"Mr. Darcy! I did not realize you had arrived. Please, come in!" Elizabeth tried to cover her embarrassment. 'What can he mean stealing in on me, disapprobation written so clearly across his face?'

"Your Grace," he stammered and bowed. "Forgive me. I... I was lost in thought..." 'seeing you there, with your son... literally stole my breath away,' ran through his head. What emerged from his mouth was a stilted, "A moment of your time, madam?"

"Of course." Elizabeth rang for Rafael's nurse, who quickly accepted the boy in her waiting arms. When the door closed behind them, Elizabeth began, "Did you have a pleasant journey, sir?"

"Yes, quite. Your Grace, thank you for accommodating me."

"It is I who should thank you, for allowing Georgiana to remain with us."

"Forgive me, how is your father?"

"Passably well. Dr. Grimwald visits him, but at present his recovery is all we could hope for."

Darcy nodded, unsure if Elizabeth was satisfied with this outcome. "At least you are able to provide him with the best medical care..."

"*Money* can... provide, Mr. Darcy?"

"Yes, quite." He coughed uncomfortably, unhappy with the tone and direction of the conversation. "How do you fare, Eliza... your Grace?" he asked quietly.

Surprised, Elizabeth drew back, unprepared for such a sensible and sensitively placed question. Darcy continued, the words speeding ahead of his thoughts, "I ask with more than a passing fancy. You aware that Rafael asked that I take care of his sons?" Elizabeth gasped indicating her surprise at his declaration.

"You, you would take them?" she whispered not able to believe what was happening around her.

"And you," he added softly. Elizabeth opened her mouth to speak, but no words emerged. She closed it and was about to speak again, but Darcy pressed forward trying to convince her of his devotion, of what he was willing to endure for her sake. "I understand how people will speak of… about the impropriety… of our arrangement."

"Arrangement? Of what do you speak, Mr. Darcy?" Elizabeth's eyes registered his looking at her as if she were a child.

"You and I, your Grace."

"I beg your pardon, sir, but …"

Darcy interrupted her. "Your Grace, Rafael charged me with your well being…" Darcy had not expected her resistance, and his anger burned at this defiance of his desire.

"Mr. Darcy! For nearly four months we… There has been no word from you, no support, no guidance. Yet, we still have a roof over our head and food upon our table. Your interference at this juncture is unwarranted, and unwelcome and I beg you to…"

"Rafael demanded my promise…"

"I fully appreciate this, I have received your offer…"

"To marry…"

"And I release you…. Marry?" she took a step back as if he had slapped her. He stood opposite her, frozen, his mind reeling at her rejection. His mouth hung open, and his hands fell meekly to his side. Her voice rang through his confusion, rousing him to attend to her words. "Did you honestly say… do you believe that such a bloodless discussion would induce me to marry you…?" She added nearly underneath her breath, "of all people?"

Hearing her mumbled address, he straightened stiffly, his pride rekindled, "As that was the wish of your late husband, yes, yes I do."

Elizabeth paced the room. "I see." She looked at him then returned her gaze to the floor upon which she trod. Inwardly, she counted to ten, and then again before being able to calm her thoughts and guide her tongue into a civil response. 'I knew it!' she shot him a resentful glance. 'Insufferable man! He thinks he can just come in here and order me about, as if I have no say in the matter as I am not born into this sphere. Of all the… the… the conceit of the man,' she glanced angrily over at him again. He had the decency to blush and look away as her head whipped back to look at the floor. 'What unmitigated gall… such pride… hateful man.' Her arms crossed in front of her as she walked to the fireplace. Tapping her toe on the hearth she again tried to order her thoughts. Pinching her arms, she suddenly turned to face him, straightening her gown she spoke. "I am afraid I must refuse your request, Mr. Darcy. I am not in need of a keeper, especially not one who has never harbored a good opinion of me."

"Your Grace…"

Elizabeth held up her hand to silence him. "I appreciate the *sacrifice* you are willing to make, but I cannot, will not marry a man I wholeheartedly dis… let me just say, I thank you, but no." She was finding it increasingly difficult to control her temper, so she paced.

"I thought…" her rejection burned in his voice.

She stopped, and turning slowly towards him, her eyes blazed. She spoke slowly, very slowly. "You thought what exactly, sir?"

"That you would welcome my offer," he scrambled to put his incoherent thoughts in order. "I am a suitable prospect…"

"Prospect? Enough, Mr. Darcy! I believe it best to end this conversation before we say things that will strain our acquaintance beyond its breaking point. I would not do that to either Georgiana or Agatha. As for myself, you are the last man on Earth I would *ever* marry!"

Struck dumb, Darcy just stood there.

"If you will excuse me, I must see Mrs. Nelson about dinner."

Elizabeth left the room as quickly as she could. Darcy remained standing, unsure how things had descended so quickly into disaster.

Darcy kept to his rooms for the majority of the evening and the next day, emerging only at meals, at which he was unduly silent. Georgiana could not coax a word from him, and kept looking to Dame Agatha for reassurance. Unfortunately, Elizabeth had not confided in her, and while not clueless to the general nature of the discussion, she was unwilling to speculate. The day after, while Elizabeth was with Georgiana and the boys, Darcy was summoned for an unexpected, private audience with Agatha. Finding her in the solarium, Darcy took in the tableau, the older woman looking out of the glass, watching Elizabeth and Georgiana help the boys in their attempts to stand. Together they observed the young women bending toward the toddlers, each holding one child upright, aiding them in their first steps. Their squeals, squawks and giggles could be heard echoing about the large, airy room.

"Agatha?" Darcy said, wanting to confess his blunder, but unsure where and how to begin.

"I am glad you came," silence filled the room as Darcy chastised himself. Agatha turned to face the man she had loved since he was a boy. "Do not hide yourself, William."

"I believe I have done just the opposite! I have exposed myself, brutally."

She raised an eyebrow at him. He raked his hand through his hair, his eye catching Elizabeth giggling as she picked up her son who now sat on his bottom with a quivering smile. As she drew the child to her breast, kisses raining down on his head and cheek, Darcy sighed. "All I wanted was for her..."

"To come, and be your mistress." Agatha finished his thought.

He bristled indignantly. "I asked for her hand."

"With as much respect and compassion as one would for the former." Darcy's blush overshadowed his hauteur. "At least that is how Elizabeth perceived it." Darcy turned to glare at Agatha. "You spoke of your eligibility, your worth in the opinion of the *ton*, as if you and Rafe were interchangeable." Agatha took a deep breath trying to quell the anger unexpectedly rising in her heart. "My nephew asked for you to care for his family, Fitzwilliam, not disparage them into submission."

"I did not mean to..."

"Well, meaning to or not, that is what you have accomplished." She looked out at the quartet approaching the house. "The question remains, what you are willing to do about it."

~

As dawn lit the sky, Darcy found Elizabeth strolling through the roses in one of her gardens. "Your Grace?" he called out, quickly closing the distance between them. Turning, Elizabeth saw the tall man stride across the lawn, steeling herself for the encounter.

"Mr. Darcy," she replied coolly. He continued in silence wondering how he had made it this far.

"Your Grace," he repeated, watching her defenses rise. "Please," his hand reached out for her. She stiffened. He withdrew, bringing both arms to clasp behind his back. "I wish to apologize for any... misconceptions my remarks from the other day may have caused." He looked away at the trees. "I do not wish to remove you or your boys from Crystalglen. Nor force your... anything upon you. I could not..." he turned to look at her again. "No one could force you against your will... against your heart. I have misjudged and misconstrued my role, entirely. But it is not solely out of pride, nor obligation to Rafe."

She quirked her brow at this. "No?" While unable to discharge her anger, she was curious where he was taking the conversation.

He hesitated. "No, not solely." He looked down then spoke, the words rushing through his lips. "I have feelings... deep feelings for you that compel me, your Grace. The same feelings that demand I come and humble myself before you. I ask... am begging for the chance to... appropriately... to court you... as is your due, as a woman well worth pleasing."

She looked skeptically at him.

"I would wish to begin anew, if possible. Perhaps when we meet next in town, my sister and I may call upon you, and Agatha? And the children?"

She began walking. Taking a few steps she stopped, turned and looked at Darcy. Seeing his uncertainty, her heart began to soften. "I make no promises, sir."

"I expect none."

A slight small smile brightened her countenance, banishing the gloom from his heart. He offered his arm and after only a moment's hesitation, she took it.

Together they returned to the house where Agatha, Georgiana, and the children awaited.

⁓

Nearly a week later, Darcy found himself pleasantly ensconced with his sister in the solarium where she worked on a watercolor of the flowers Elizabeth had arranged. "I know Elizabeth wrote you, William, but I wish to tell you… what happened… myself."

"Dearest, we need not revisit this…"

"Yes, we must." Georgiana looked directly at her brother, her back straight, her countenance firm.

"As you wish," he put down the book he was reading.

"I was wrong to entertain the notion of eloping, Brother. I see that now. Even if…" here she stumbled. Darcy turned his head, unable to witness her distress. As he was about to rise from his chair he felt her hand hold him firmly in place. He turned to see her looking directly at him. "Even if Mr. Wickham loved me, which I no longer believe is the case, to elope would be wrong. If love is not strong enough to present in the light of day, it is not love." Georgiana took a deep breath before taking her brother's hand in hers. "I am sorry, William, if my foolishness caused you grief, sorrow," she hesitated. "Or shame. However, I am grateful for the experience. I have learned how lonely I was, how my grief for our father had isolated me, leaving me ripe for one such as he. I am no longer that lonely child. I have found friendship and acceptance with people who love me, as I am. This is enough, for now." A small smile lifted her lips, "Until a true beau presents himself."

Darcy groaned, but was inwardly pleased with his sister's speech.

Their conversation turned to Pemberley and the latest antics of their relations, until Agatha found them. "Georgiana, Darcy, there you are." Darcy rose and bowed. "I am glad you have had time together, and I wish to thank you both for Georgiana's time with us. I know not what we would do without you, my dear." Georgiana blushed, prettily. "But now, I wish a word with your brother."

"Of course. Where is Elizabeth?"

"Where else? With the boys. They woke from their nap, demanding their mamma!"

Kissing her brother on the cheek, she merrily replied, "I am off to play soldier, or is it horsey, with the young men of my heart."

"If you wait for one of them to come of age, I will gladly give my consent." Darcy quipped back at her.

"Droll, brother. Very droll." Georgiana deadpanned before skipping off to find the children.

Agatha chuckled as she took her seat. Darcy sat beside her.

"Thank you, Dame Agatha, for all you…"

"And Elizabeth…"

"And the Duchess, have done for my sister." He could not yet say her name.

"Nonsense, man. She is like a daughter to me."

"Thank you," he placed his hand on hers and bending, kissed her cheek.

"You are welcome, William." She took a deep breath and steeled her expression. "I wish to speak with you of a more… unpleasant matter, William."

His head shot up, his eyes narrowed. He nodded.

"You are aware that Elizabeth travelled to Ramsgate yesterday?"

Despite his best attempts, Darcy stiffened at the mention of a place linked in his mind to infamy. He nodded, recalling the emptiness that had filled him knowing she was gone. Pressing estate business precluded his accompanying her into the seaside town. "She had business there, with the magistrate, and was of course, escorted … heavily escorted," she leaned in for emphasis. "And thank heavens she was!"

Darcy's attention was riveted to his companion, a sense of foreboding growing in his heart. Agatha looked seriously at Darcy who added. "Wickham is in Ramsgate. His affair with Miss King, it seems came to a premature conclusion." Agatha looked questioningly at him.

He shrugged. "My agent informed me of his return, and her uncle of his character."

Agatha added, "That explains a great deal." Now it was Darcy's turn for confusion. "Wickham was still loitering about Elisabeth's carriage." Darcy gripped the edge of his chair. "He had been drowning his disappointment at losing both Georgiana and Miss King." Darcy leapt out of the chair, pacing as with dread seriousness, Agatha continued. "He approached Elizabeth, inquiring as to the whereabouts of your sister. Elizabeth told him in no uncertain terms, he was to stay away from her, or he would have the house of Gainsbridge, as well as you to contend with." Darcy's eyes flared. "Elizabeth made light of the entire incident when I mentioned it to her, after Georgiana had retired of course. She was vexed that I knew of it at all."

Surprise fueled his question. "If El… her Grace did not speak of it, how…?"

"Elizabeth's escort was suitably shaken by Wickham's demeanor, and the way he looked at Elizabeth as she turned to leave. He had grabbed her by the arm…"

Darcy growled. Agatha noted his reaction, but continued. "Dorsley said she froze and looked at Wickham, telling him to unhand her. Wickham only increased the pressure until he looked into her eyes. Even though her guards closed round her, it was what he found there that drained the gumption out of him, and he released her. Elizabeth returned to the carriage and they made haste out of town."

"I will kill him…" Darcy spat.

Agatha rose to join him. She patted his arm. "You shall do no such thing! Georgiana needs you, and I know you have other promises to keep." She looked at his blank expression until recognition returned. He sighed. She tried to repress the chuckle that threatened to bubble up from her breast. He sighed again, and Agatha could not contain herself. She shook her head giggling. "William, William, William, you have so much to learn." He looked at her as if she had grown a second head. "Give her time, my young, headstrong friend." With that she left the room.

ത

Dinner that evening was strained with Georgiana and Agatha watching the cool, polite tones of Elizabeth, and the embarrassed overtures of Darcy. Both women had a difficult time restraining their mirth, convinced that neither party was ready to make light of the situation.

The next morning, William found Elizabeth walking the grounds, unaccompanied. "Your Grace, a moment of your time?" Elizabeth slumped her shoulders but acquiesced. He quickened his step to join her. When he was at her side, all words fled his mind. He looked at her and was caught in her eyes. They were cool, reserved and shone like diamonds, and Darcy knew they were as sharp as well. He stammered. "I… Dame Agatha informed me of your encounter with Wickham."

Elizabeth turned and began walking. He kept pace with her. "I wish to thank you, your Grace, for defending my sister in my stead." This last was said with such self-recrimination Elizabeth was moved to mercy. She stopped, turning towards him.

"Mr. Darcy, Georgiana was under *my* protection at the time. She was here at *my* behest to serve *my* need. While I appreciate your thanks, truly I do," she reached for his arm, her fingers sensing the muscles underneath his coat. He froze as fire sparked his blood. Elizabeth was similarly affected and for a moment she could not speak. Their eyes met; confusion met passion. Elizabeth was the first to pull away. She spoke in a whisper. "There is no need to speak any more about it. Georgiana is like a sister to me. Her company is a great comfort."

"I am happy you feel so." Darcy's voice was heavy with emotion. "I know she adores Agatha, and your sons. You are like a sister to her. And to me..." there was so much he wished to say.

"We should return to the house. The boys will be up soon, and I promised them a romp." She hurried along, unwilling to hear his declaration. He caught up with her.

"El... your Grace... You must know..." He collected the thoughts his heart cried out to make. "I am at your disposal, your Grace. I will be the father your children have been denied... if you allow." 'And the husband that has been taken from you,' he added in his heart, unable to voice what he knew was true. He reached for her hand and they stood there, neither willing, nor able to break away. It was Georgiana and the boys calling for her that broke the bond that held them where they stood. Elizabeth looked toward the approaching commotion, then back at him and nodded. "I will think on it," she said before breaking the connection and scurrying off toward her family.

Elizabeth paced in the master's chambers. Since her husband's death, she had returned to the Mistress' chambers to sleep alone. Tonight, though, she wished to revisit the pleasant memories that had for so long evaded her. Yet every time she tried to recall his touch, his taste, the feel of his skin upon her own in the most intimate of embraces, she could not. Instead of the silken waves of gold that adorned Rafael's head, the dark curls of his friend, Fitzwilliam Darcy, intruded and her breath grew rapid and shallow. Her skin tingled, recalling the feel of his muscle beneath her fingertips.

'He is such a man, a complicated, live man,' she thought as her fingers brushed the exposed flesh of her neck. 'Those eyes!' She shuddered, recalling the first time she had seen him stare at her while she danced at the Granby's ball. 'So intense! What a fool I am,' she scoffed, 'believing I could take on one such as he.' She stopped, her hand resting on her collarbone. 'And yet,' and her mind filled with images of those strong arms embracing her. There in her dead husband's bed chamber, her feelings of disloyalty were challenged, and when Elizabeth went to bed, pleasant thoughts ran through the battlefield her mind had become.

That night, however, Elizabeth dreamt of Rafael, not Darcy, reliving all their moments of marital bliss. In her dream he was alive and eager for her. As the dream came to its end, Elizabeth saw him standing, his shirt undone, his clothing haphazardly repositioned, his eyes sorrowful as he gazed upon her and faded into the grey of the dawn.

~

Elizabeth and Darcy negotiated their way through the remainder of their visit. A week went by before Darcy was granted another private audience with Elizabeth. She had sent word she wished to see him in the study before he retired. With trepidation he answered her summons, unnerved with anxiety. The intervening days had been pleasant, with Elizabeth ever the polite hostess. But there was never time for private discussion, even though he noted with pleasure the lengths she allowed him to know her children. They were growing, learning to walk, and babbling. Ian was even formulating rudimentary words. Both boys appeared to comprehend what was said around them, and at times were quiet and pensive. This was often right before they exploded into mischief as when they scooted to the sidebar opening cabinets to explore the crystal and porcelain.

Then there was the time Maria caught them just as they were about to excavate in her Grace's chamber pot. Darcy delighted in their antics, forming a picture of his friend as a young boy, and what their mother was like as a child. The liberality she bestowed upon her children, allowing them to explore, under supervision of course, and the amount of time she herself spent with them reading, or drawing or walking gave him an inkling of the bounty of her nature. He marveled at the open, trusting joy with which both Ian and Rafael greeted those in their intimate circle. For Darcy, it added to his determination to win her and cement his place in their world. That he was not shunned even though he knew his behavior and previous judgment deserved just that, encouraged him in his desire.

He was startled when the door opened, and Agatha faced him. She smirked at his confusion, before standing on her tiptoes to place a kiss on his cheek. "All will be well, William," she patted his cheek. "You will see." Still stunned at being caught at Elizabeth's door, Darcy stood, blinking. Agatha chuckled and left. He entered the room, rapping his knuckles against the wood.

Elizabeth turned from across the room where she had been staring out at the moon lit lawn. "Mr. Darcy."

He entered the room with an iota more of confidence. He smiled timidly, and she beamed back at him. At that moment, Fitzwilliam Darcy was a lost man. It was the smile he had coveted for two years. The one he had first seen at the Granby ball, the one she had kept for Rafael alone. His heart constricted at the thought, and he pulled back his emotion. Noting his withdrawal, Elizabeth dimmed her smile in response. He felt bereft, forlorn, and longed for the return of its radiance.

"Your Grace," he spoke. "Forgive me. I was overcome by your beauty, yet again. I thought, for a moment... that you welcomed me."

Confused, Elizabeth continued. "I do, Mr. Darcy. I do. Did I not seek an audience with you?" Her eyes twinkled and her lips twitched at his discomposure.

He nodded.

"Please, come, let us sit." She came forward and motioned for him to sit in one of a pair of armchairs.

"I have given your offer great thought, sir," she began. Darcy's heart flushed with anticipation and hope. "I realize… Agatha has subsequently informed me of the substance of your last conversation with Rafael... I was unaware he had spoken to you… of such matters." She looked down at her hands, gaining time to order her thoughts. "It is true… my sons will need a male influence in their lives… as they grow. I have no brothers, only sisters. I would be pleased and honored for you to be that man in their lives."

Darcy sat waiting for her to continue, to address the matter of most importance to his heart. While she remained silent, his fear grew stronger. "And you, milady?"

"Me?"

His eyes never left her while he nodded. "Yes, you. You were part of that promise."

"I… no… no, I am not part of any promise, Mr. Darcy. I…" she looked away before whispering, "it is too soon… Rafael is not yet gone a year," she quickly stood and began pacing in front of him. With tears in her eyes, she stopped, then quickly curtsied and departed, leaving a disappointed Darcy to pick up the pieces of his heart.

~

The Darcys departed the next morning. Agatha and the boys were sad to say goodbye. While Elizabeth had tears in her eyes as she embraced Georgiana, she was nearly composed in her farewell to Darcy.

"I will send word of the boys," she began, a sweet smile on her lips, but Darcy noted, it did not reach her eyes. He brought her hand to his lips, but said nothing, only nodded in acknowledgment. "Goodbye, Mr. Darcy. May you have a safe journey."

"Thank you, your Grace. Until we meet again."

Reluctantly letting her hand slide from his, he turned and climbed into the coach. Steeling himself not to turn and look back as did his sister, Darcy focused on stemming the tears overflowing his heart.

൜

With only her family at Crystalglen Elizabeth found herself lonely. She continued her solitary rambles which, more often than not, led to the family graveyard and to the crypt of her husband. She would rest there, on the marble bench staring at the tomb holding his remains. It was the one place where she felt calm, where she would retreat to when the boys became too much, too insistent for her attention. When she wanted time to think her thoughts in solitude, the still silence gave her comfort. As she sat, tears pooled together until they fell, one by one down her rosy cheek. She sat, staring at the sarcophagi, willing Rafael to return, 'to take away this emptiness. I do not want to leave you, Rafe,' she thought. 'But I cannot continue like this. It hurts too much. He is here, and the boys, and I … I wish him to remain. I am sorry… husband… Rafael, but I will choose another… not now… but soon.'

Elizabeth sat listening to the sounds of nature around her, the birds in the trees, the wind dancing with the leaves and could almost believe she did not exist as a separate entity, but as part of the magnificent whole. In moments such as these, she felt her spirit rise, expanding beyond the limits of her body, the limits of her station, melding into the peace and greatness of Nature. There, in that moment of release she opened her heart unguardedly, offering it as it was, in all its pain and imperfection, she felt free, whole, at peace. In that moment hope grew.

~ CHAPTER SIX ~

October 1811
Purvis Lodge, Hertfordshire

That autumn Elizabeth leased the estate of Purvis Lodge near her ancestral home of Longbourn. While no longer in formal mourning, her heart remained heavy and she hungered for the comfort of her family. Her father had not returned to health and the burden of maintaining the estate fell increasingly on Jane and Elizabeth wanted to be of assistance. As her coach rode past Netherfield, her breath caught, and pain stabbed her heart. "Rafael," she said, her fingers caressing the glass as the horses ambled on.

"Mamma," Ian called his mother back to the present, away from memories that brought sadness to her eyes. "There 'et?" the little boy asked, clambering onto her lap. She clasped his tiny frame to her chest, burying her head in his dark curls.

"Almost my sweetling, almost. Look, there!" Elizabeth pointed out the opposite window. "That is where Mamma grew up."

"Mamma?" asked Rafael from across the seat where he sat with Dame Agatha.

"Yes, my love?" she asked, her head perched on Ian's.

"Taunt Janie?" he asked as he pressed his nose to the glass.

Elizabeth laughed, realizing that it was the first time she had spontaneously done so in a very long while. "Yes, you little imp, we shall see *Taunt Janie* very soon. And Grandmamma, and all your aunts." Elizabeth smiled and looking up caught the eye of Dame Agatha.

"It does me good to see you smile, Elizabeth. It has been too long." Elizabeth darkened momentarily, until she gathered herself to look back at her aunt.

"Yes indeed, Agatha." Wishing to distract the conversation, Elizabeth regaled her companions with tales of her childhood scampering among the trees and meadows in search of wildlife and flowers. Shortly, the carriages passed through Meryton, amazing all who walked the streets by their splendor and the ducal crest. Elizabeth turned her head, hiding the smile playing upon her lips.

Soon they were ensconced in Purvis Lodge, with Mrs. Bates putting her charges down for a nap. Agatha and Elizabeth adjourned to one of the many drawing rooms that best caught the afternoon light. The duchess had sent word to her family of their arrival, inviting them to dine the next afternoon. However, as Mrs. Stemple brought in tea, unexpected guests were announced.

"Mrs. Bennet, Miss Bennet, Miss Mary, Catherine and Lydia Bennet, ma'am."

The women rose to greet Elizabeth's family.

"Lizzy!" Mrs. Bennet screeched. Elizabeth winced, praying that the children would not wake from their nap. "Where are you hiding my grandsons? Why are they not here to greet me?"

"Mamma, they are resting. The journey here was too exciting for them to sleep in the carriage."

"Mrs. Bennet, how nice of you to call *so* soon." Agatha offered her hand to Mrs. Bennet, who upon seeing the Duchess, bowed formally, momentarily chagrined at her earlier outburst.

"Dame Agatha! How splendid to see you. Elizabeth did not mention that you were to join us."

"Mamma, I said I would bring my family," Elizabeth whispered. Mrs. Bennet bristled at Agatha's designation as family, secretly coveting Elizabeth's return so she could determine how best to spend the Gainsbridge fortune. The two elder women eyed each other, both standing their ground.

"Lizzy, I am so glad you are here," Jane interrupted the rising tension by embracing her sister. "We have missed you so."

The rest of the afternoon was spent reminiscing and catching up on local gossip until the boys rose from their nap. They were eager to run, and the entire party headed out of doors for a ramble on the estate. The children were ecstatic to find they had aunts young enough to run and play. In addition to Jane tending to their every whim, the boys found Aunt Lydia to be vastly amusing. She would chase them, and sweep them up in her arms, laughing and tickling them until their eyes became heavy from the exertion and the crisp, fresh air.

The most interesting news to Elizabeth's ear was that Mr. Bingley had leased Netherfield, and upon hearing of the Bennet's connection to the Duchess of Deronshire, had been eager to further the acquaintance. Elizabeth was quite pleased at her sister's blushes as Jane related their first meeting at the assembly nearly a month ago, and that they had subsequently engaged in conversation at the many social events local society provided.

Two days later, Elizabeth was upset to receive a note informing her that Jane had caught a chill the night of her dinner with Mr. Bingley's sisters. Although nothing was explicitly said, Elizabeth knew enough of Jane to know she would appreciate a friendly face during her convalescence. Leaving her children in the capable care of Agatha and Mrs. Bates, Elizabeth saddled her horse and rode the five miles to Netherfield.

At the stables, Elizabeth discovered she was not alone in her desire for an early morning ride. There, stabling his magnificent stallion, Fitzwilliam Darcy stood, open-mouthed as he watched her draw near the waiting groomsman.

"Your Grace," he said, barely above a whisper. The groom approached to help her dismount, but he waved the boy away.

"Mr. Darcy," she said hesitantly as he lifted his arms to guide her descent. His eyes followed hers as she slid gracefully down the side of her horse, his hands burning into her skin as they pressed along her waist. He felt his cheeks flush and his blood stir his loins. Even if he had wished it, his eyes could not but drink in her beauty, starved as they were by the many months he had been denied her presence.

"Thank you," she said softly when she was again safely on the ground.

"What brings you to Netherfield? Not that you are unwelcome, it is just..."

Biting back the smile that played upon her lips, Elizabeth responded, "My sister, Jane?" Darcy stood, mute, unable to think while his hands still possessed her body. Elizabeth continued, flustered by the feel of him upon her. "She has taken a chill. I wish to see her, if I may."

"Of course. Allow me?" He offered his arm and as she looked up at him, she took in as much of him as she could. After a moment's hesitation, she accepted and together, they walked to the main house.

Inside, Charles Bingley was sincere in his welcome. "How kind of you to attend your sister, your Grace. This way, please." The gentlemen escorted the Duchess to her sister's chamber, before Caroline Bingley had even roused from bed. Elizabeth hoped Jane would be awake to receive her, but the pallor of her skin, and the look of concern on the maid who sat with the invalid, unnerved her. With a glance, Elizabeth indicated her desire to speak with Mr. Bingley outside of Jane's chamber. Once he, Darcy and Elizabeth left the room, she began.

"Mr. Bingley, I wonder if I may ask that you send for Mr. Ashton, the apothecary? He is very knowledgeable, and I believe his services would greatly benefit my sister." She looked back at the door. Her lower lip caught between her teeth as she pondered how much to reveal to the gentlemen. "My sister… has taken on much of the burden of running the estate, since my father… he has not been well, you see."

"Of course, your Grace. Say no more. I shall send a note requesting he attend to Miss Bennet, immediately."

Elizabeth smiled. "Thank you, Mr. Bingley. And now, if you will excuse me, I will stay with Jane until Mr. Ashton arrives."

"Of course, your Grace." He said, bowing gracefully.

"Your Grace," Darcy echoed his friend in motion and speech. She bowed her head in recognition before escaping into her sister's chamber.

After Caroline Bingley and Mrs. Hurst had breakfasted, they made their way to the invalid's chamber. Their progress was halted by the arrival of Mr. Ashton. His examination prohibited visiting until after the supper hour, as there were draughts to administer, and then the patient's need to rest. Near teatime, Elizabeth joined the Bingleys and their guest in the drawing room.

"Your Grace, how is your sister?" Mr. Bingley inquired.

A slight frown crossed Elizabeth's brow. "I am as yet uncertain, sir. She rests, but her fever has not completely abated."

"Oh, my dear!" Caroline Bingley simpered. "How dreadful! To think the poor girl came on horseback in the rain. What ever could she have been thinking?" she asked in disbelief while her posture and glance indicated a disdainful prejudice against their latest arrival and her family.

"Caroline!" Bingley interjected.

"The squall took us *all* by surprise, Miss Bingley." Mr. Darcy added. "It was only luck that we arrived at the officers' quarters before the rains began." The look he gave his hostess would have quelled a more observant soul. However, Miss Bingley was less than astute at reading emotional subtext, seeing and hearing only what she desired.

Elizabeth's eyes narrowed as she watched Miss Bingley react to the censure of Mr. Bingley and his friend. Then she looked at the gentlemen themselves. Charles Bingley left no doubt in her mind of his disgust with his sister's behavior. The other gentleman was more inscrutable. Darcy's eyes held disdain for the rude outburst they had all witnessed, but when his eyes turned to Elizabeth, for a moment they turned soft as a caress, before becoming a shield effectively barring her from probing deeper. She nodded and said as she turned, "I will find a book from your library, Mr. Bingley," he nodded his acquiescence, "and return to my sister. If you will excuse me?"

She left the group at the bottom of the stairs, heading to the library. Darcy waited a full ten minutes before succumbing to temptation. He walked as steadily as he could to the library, his heart beating faster at each step. Collecting himself he placed his hand on the handle and turned it, opening to a sight he had only dreamt of. There stood Elizabeth in the growing dusk, by the bookshelf perusing a volume of poetry. The fire cast a warm glow on her skin as she stood in profile. He drank in her silhouetted figure, admiring her curves and the delicacy of her fingers as she turned a page. He almost gasped, noting how her lower lip caught between her teeth. Without thinking he spoke his voice a whisper of longing. "Have you found what you desire, your Grace?"

Her head flew up as her eyes opened wide, her teeth released her lip, and Darcy could just make out how it darkened with the flush of returning blood. She licked her lips before speaking. "I… it is… Blake…"

"Ah," he said moving stealthily closer. Due to his long legs he was directly in front of her in five steps. She took a step back, until the bookshelf intruded and she tipped forward. Darcy stepped in to hold her, rewarded by her breast brushing against his chest. He could not stop himself, and he drew her toward his body, allowing gravity to propel her into his embrace. "Elizabeth," he murmured, lowering his lips to her hair. He inhaled the scent of lavender into his lungs and sighed. "How long I have waited for this," he whispered into the curls piled on top of her head. "Please, tell me there is hope."

"Mr. Darcy! Release me!" she pushed him back, but he held her to him as if clinging to life. Mortification flushed each face.

"I cannot, Elizabeth, please! Do not ask this of me." His voice was full of a deep longing, a well of sorrow from which he reached out to her. She took a step back, until the shelving against the wall forced her to move forward again. Elizabeth, in order to steady herself, clasped her hands to his arms, holding him. He felt her steady herself, but she did not release him. Quickly he focused on her face, seeing her flushed cheek, hearing her breath hitch as she looked up at him, not to his eyes but his lips. His heart rejoiced.

The door was heard to open, and he quickly released her from his grasp. She stepped back, taking the book. "Good evening, sir," she said coldly leaving the room as Mr. Bingley entered.

"Your Grace, your sister calls for you," Bingley said, taking hold of her hands, anxiously. "Please, come, I will bring you to her."

"Thank you, sir. Let us go straight away."

The door closed, leaving Darcy with a fire raging within his breast. He stumbled to the mantle, unable to untangle her image from his mind. His body retained the physical sensation of her pressed into it, and a rare smile graced his face. He stood until he heard the bell announcing it was time to dress for dinner and he left for his room, all the while thinking of ways to regain the exclusive company of this intoxicating woman.

~

Darcy paced his room like a caged animal. The afternoon's foray into courting the widow Elizabeth replayed itself endlessly in his mind. He had had to relieve himself twice already that evening, his body anticipating how their next encounter might unfold. 'Surely she will dine with us,' he thought as he nervously fidgeted with the knot of his cravat. She had taken tea in her sister's chambers earlier in the day, disappointing Darcy tremendously.

~

At dinner the next evening, Caroline attacked. Lady Evelyn Gladstone, a known friend of the Duchess Gainsbridge was embroiled in a grand scandal involving the Viscount Malcolm O'Donnell, an Irish nobleman who had fallen for her charms and had imposed himself upon her in a public manner.

"Duchess," she began as the soup had been served, "I have received a letter from my friend in town, Miss Ellerton," she surveyed the eyes of those sitting at her table. "She claims that Lady Gladstone will be excluded from Almack's for..."

"I believe Lady Gladstone," interrupted Darcy, "will be vindicated when her true relationship with Lord O'Donnell is revealed."

Caroline blanched as she stammered. "Oh?"

"Yes," continued Elizabeth. "She and Lord O'Donnell were wed a month ago."

"Impossible!" Caroline insisted. "She still resides at Gladstone Manor."

"I believe that is because," Darcy commanded, "Lady Evelyn returned to her grandmother's sickbed. Lord O'Donnell was detained in Dublin, but returned as soon as he was able. If Lady Margaret was not so ill, there would be no hint of scandal, for the news of their marriage would have disseminated among the *ton* by less scurrilous means." He glared at Caroline whose mouth flapped like a gasping fish.

"But to marry in Ireland, of all places?" she was not conceding without a fight. "Their choice makes Meryton appear a bastion of civilization."

"Yes, well, I believe that was the bride's choice to accommodate her groom. The Earl of Montglen is rather ill, and would not have been able to attend the marriage of his only child, and heir," Darcy added. "I myself stood as Malcolm's witness for the ceremony."

The smile that Elizabeth gave to Darcy ignited his hope even further. She added, "The letter I received from Lady Ellerton recounted the ceremony, but neglected to mention the guests who attended..."

"Her eyes were for Lord Malcolm, only," Darcy smiled at Elizabeth's blush.

The arrival of the servants with the next course cast a pall in the conversation. Caroline watched with growing ire as Elizabeth and Darcy exchanged looks full of hidden meaning. She sat, reviewing her tactics. When the diners were again alone she pounced. "Your Grace?" she began, holding Elizabeth in her gaze until the woman looked her in the eye. With all eyes upon her, Caroline continued. "Miss Ellerton has also heard that many ask when *you* will return to society. She says that the gentlemen in particular eagerly await your return to society."

Darcy stiffened, Caroline gloated and Elizabeth set her flatware on the table. After wiping her lips on the linen napkin, Elizabeth looked Caroline directly in the eye. "While my husband was alive, and... well enough..." she took a deep breath while clasping her hands together on her lap, "We would often open our home to the philosophers and artists of London. Many members of society came to our home for evenings of conversation and... good company."

"I am sure that is not..." Caroline attempted.

Darcy interjected, "I, along with my cousin, Fitzwilliam, and his father, the Earl of Matlock were fortunate to attend a number of these evenings at Wyndom House. I, too, eagerly await your return to town, your Grace, and add my request that you, and Dame Agatha continue to host these evenings. I know, I along with my family, will do all we may to help reinstate them. We only await your invitation."

Again Darcy was graced by a radiant smile from Elizabeth. Charles entered the conversation, changing the topic to plans for returning to London. From there they spoke of the theater and composers they anticipated hearing in the coming year. After the meal was over, Elizabeth excused herself to check on Jane's comfort.

~

The next evening, despite her better judgment, Elizabeth forced herself to partake of dinner with the family. With polite replies to all, she sat where she was guided, near Mr. Hurst and Mr. Bingley. To her relief, Mr. Darcy was seated at the opposite end of the table, surrounded by Miss Bingley and Mrs. Hurst. Conversation remained within the bounds of civility through the first course, but by the second, Caroline could no longer stand the unrestrained glances Darcy continually sent towards the Duchess.

"So, your Grace," she simpered darkly, "Have you decided when you will return for the coming season?"

Elizabeth looked sharply to her left, scrutinizing the tone and hostility she found in the woman's eyes. "Yes, Miss Bingley, I have." Despite his best attempt, Darcy could not restrain his eagerness to hear her reply. "Dame Agatha has requested that we travel to town after the holidays."

"As has my sister," Darcy added, looking directly at Elizabeth.

"How lovely for you," Caroline drawled. She took another sip of wine, inwardly seething at the attention that should be hers. "Mr. Darcy, shall you join us in time for Twelfth Night?"

Pulling his eyes from Elizabeth, he slowly turned to his hostess. "Whether or not we return that soon, I cannot say. No one may predict the weather. But," his eyes returned to Elizabeth. I hope to, as soon as may be, Miss Bingley. Georgiana and I shall spend the holidays... with my aunt and uncle..." Caroline's face dropped as did her hope for a holiday invitation to Pemberley. "By then I am sure she will wish to visit with their Graces, Lords Ian and Rafael..."

Elizabeth chuckled at hearing her children so addressed.

"What amuses you, your Grace?" Caroline asked, repulsed at the idea of being laughed at.

"To hear my scamps so reverentially referred to, 'tis all."

"They are near on a year, are they not?" Louisa Hurst asked. Elizabeth nodded. "I have always had a weak spot for children," she said, eyeing her husband longingly. He caught her glance before sipping his wine, and nodded imperceptibly before lifting his glass in her direction. Elizabeth looked at Louisa's blush and smiled wondering if the Hursts would soon have an announcement to make regarding a happy addition to their family.

"I received a letter this afternoon," Caroline advanced returning everyone's attention to herself, "from my friend Miss Gloria Ellis. She recounts that the Duchess of Nottingham was caught in a scandal of sorts. She is a known friend of yours, is she not?"

Elizabeth flushed. She too, had received word from Deborah Glouster, how the Earl of Saxonby had tried to compromise her. She had been forced to retreat to her family home until the gossip dissipated. Taking a moment to focus her thoughts, Elizabeth turned to face Caroline, surprised at the look of pure malice gleaming on her angular features. Elizabeth shuddered. "Idle speculation has never served anyone, Miss Bingley."

"Surely you would know, your Grace, whether or not it is true or the degree to which the speculation is idle."

"My friend is a woman of honor, madam. However, the gentlemen of her sphere often resort to unseemly means to obtain that which they desire."

Darcy looked abashed, wondering how much of her statement dealt with his own behavior. He wondered what the details of the situation were, and how they reflected on Elizabeth.

"The way I hear the story told is that the lady was more than willing…"

"Than I would consider the source of your information, madam. If you will excuse me, I believe I shall go and see to my sister."

Darcy looked after her with hunger, while Caroline assessed her man. Returning his attention to the others in the room, he missed the knowing assessment she made of him before turning her gaze to her sister.

∾

"Caroline, please, do not run!" Louisa muttered as she tried to keep up with her sister's longer legs.

"Louisa, keep apace," Caroline hissed back at her sluggish sister. She turned her head, on the look out for her quarry. "There he is!" 'Most likely looking for the duchess Eliza,' she silently huffed. As she came up behind the hedge row separating them, she slowed her pace, waiting for Louisa. Before Mrs. Hurst could speak or chastise her for her haste, Caroline began. "'Tis true, Louisa, Miss Ellis says it is all about town! The Duchess is ruined! Imagine, thinking she could keep not one but two paramours at her disposal! And she nearly accomplished her deceit, but Lord Saxonby had enough and called her on it."

At the look of incredulity on her companion's face, Caroline continued, "Yes, shocking, I know. But you know, these widows, they are all alike. Believing themselves to be beyond censure. And the duchess, so celebrated for her wit, and beauty. I believe it is said she has *fine eyes.* Well those eyes will be sorely missed. I dare say no respectable house will accept her, now."

"What business is it to us, Caroline! Honestly, we do not even know the duchess."

Wishing to slap her silly sibling, Miss Bingley had to bite her tongue to keep from hissing out, "True, but as we heard last evening, the Lady Elizabeth *does...* why she admitted to us that she considers her a good friend, even. Ah, there is Charles, come, let us return."

The two women left Darcy with much to dwell upon. Relief that it was not Elizabeth of whom Bingley's sisters spoke rushed over Darcy. 'And yet, to keep such company? Two lovers?' As he concluded his stroll about the gardens, he fought against his insecurity. 'Things are beginning to come together,' he thought switching his walking cane at the bushes lining the path. 'But there was all that time with no word from her…' He stopped in his track, recalling the moment in the library. "No, she could not be playing me like some misguided youth! She is not over Rafael, 'tis all. She has said so… asked for time to heal, not love another…" Yet his insecurities gained the upper hand and Darcy returned to his haughty exterior throughout the evening's supper and entertainment. This was a Darcy that Miss Bingley knew how to handle.

Two days later, the Bennet sisters returned to Purvis Lodge.

~

Caroline Bingley was not pleased, not pleased at all. Mr. Darcy was spending entirely too much time with the '*Duchess Eliza*, and absolutely not enough with me.' "He even traipses over to Purvis Lodge cavorting with those brats she calls children," the harridan snorted to her sister. "Completely undignified. If that man did not have such… enormous assets, I would give him up entirely."

'As he would you, if not for Charles's sake' Louisa Hurst thought to herself. She then had to hide her mouth behind a raised hand, the mirth this thought engendered threatening to bubble forth in a most unladylike cackle.

"What I do not understand, Louisa, *dear,* is how that… that… chit of a girl entrapped the Duke of Deronshire in the first place! I must give her credit… she is a smart one, attaching herself to him at his weakest moment, a few years before he died." Caroline was now circling the room, like a hyena. "Just think of all that money! And a title, too, and the clever puss even produced that heir and a spare… both in one go. How convenient for her. Yes, I will give her credit for that."

"Caroline, what *are* you about?" Louisa asked, making one more valiant attempt to reign in her sister's convoluted thoughts. For her effort, her younger sister gave Mrs. Hurst such a look of disdain, a chill rushed up her spine. She looked at Caroline now walking at a slower pace, a bony finger tapping her pointy chin. Louisa squinted at her, noting the silhouette made by the sunlight streaming in the window. 'Does my mind play tricks, or does Caroline look more witch-like than usual? I must tell her to have her hair styled in another fashion. That chin!' "Caroline, my dear, I must go and see to Mr. Hurst."

"Mr. Hurst? What ever for?" Caroline snapped.

Louisa only smiled, thinking warmly of her husband's request at supper, to retire for a bit of *afternoon delight* to wipe away the taste of Caroline's vitriol. "Family matters, dear. You will understand when you find a husband," she said, adding softly to herself, '*if* you ever find a man who will have you.'

Louisa left Caroline pacing in the drawing room until Charles and Darcy came stomping in. "Ah, Caroline, there you are. I have the most wonderful news."

"We return to London, brother? That would be divine, would you not agree, Mr. Darcy?"

Bingley gave her a scathing look. "No, Caroline. *We* shall be giving a ball as soon as Mrs. Danoway has made enough white soup."

"Charles, have you taken leave of your senses? A ball? H*ere*? In the wilds of... of nowhere?"

"I would think, Caroline, that the notion of entertaining not one, but two duchesses will put quite a feather in your cap for when you *do* return to town."

Caroline was about to speak, but thought better of it, considering what her brother had said. 'And it will give me the chance to exhibit my superiority to Eliza Gainsbridge, and Mr. Darcy.' She tapped her chin. 'And to claim such an acquaintance could be beneficial...'

"Very well, Charles, a ball we shall have."

"Thank you Caroline. I will leave the details to you. Darcy and I will deliver the invitations, once you have had them made up." Darcy who had been looking approvingly at his friend, was taken aback by the last. He shot his friend a petulant look and would have complained if not in mixed company. Bingley just chuckled at him. "Come, Darcy, I fancy a game of billiards."

The gentlemen left the room, and Miss Bingley busied herself with planning *the* event she was sure, of the Meryton season.

~

Preparations for the ball kept Caroline occupied, much to the relief of Netherfield's remaining inhabitants. Darcy and Bingley rode out most mornings, often encountering the Duchess and Miss Bennet as they rode the fields and trails of Purvis Lodge. They would often accompany the women as they took in the brisk air riding alongside until one pair or the other would dismount allowing their horses to drink or nibble on the remaining grasses.

One morning, after a week of these coincidental meetings, Charles Bingley dismounted as their horses' muzzles nearly touched. "Miss Bennet, how lovely to see you this fine morning." Bingley said, taking her arm to aid in her dismount. "And you, as well, your Grace."

Elizabeth smiled at his distraction before being caught off guard by Darcy who echoed his friend by standing alongside her horse, his arms raised to receive her.

"Your Grace," he said as her feet touched the ground, their lips only a breath apart. He was overwhelmed being this near to her, almost alone. He had tried to reign in his desires, but her time at Netherfield, living under the same roof even for those few days, he found her more and more irresistible. She would ride, and he accompanied her, she would read, and he found himself in need of researching one topic or another from Bingley's sparse library. She would play at the pianoforte, and he was compelled to write his sister, requiring the light in the music room for his correspondence. She had softened in her attitude toward him, allowing him to stand or sit closer than was strictly proper. When they would walk, she took his arm. These clandestine meetings allowed their relationship to deepen and he wondered how he would survive without them. As they walked, they found themselves by Noah's Puddle, a small, clear pool of sweet water and they gave their horses opportunity to fulfill their thirst.

"I would come here as a girl, and sail boats across the pond..." Elizabeth began. "Emulating Queen Elizabeth while her navy crushed the armada." She turned away to hide the blush this revelation spread across her cheeks.

He smiled at the thought of this wild vixen scampering about, banishing the Spanish fleet from the English coast. As his mind's eye conjured the cherubic Elizabeth, loose curls abounding, the grown version sat on a large rock, quickly unhooking her boots. He stood, transfixed as she reached her hand up her skirt, to pull down and remove her stockings. His breath became labored as she lifted her skirt to her calf, and gently tested the cold waters. She shivered, then twirled in the water, flicking droplets with her toes kicking in the air. He forced himself to breathe. When some of those refreshing droplets hit his cheek, he rallied himself, and moved forward taking on his most severe growl. "You would not dare, your Grace."

Her brow arched and she laughed while sending a cascade of water his way. He dodged the waterfall, nearly successful in remaining dry, but her laughter reached his heart, opening the chambers where he had locked away his younger self. Suddenly the boy who had played in the lakes and streams of Pemberley came forward and took her hand, pulling her toward him. She gasped as he held her tightly against his body, and time seemed to stand still. It no longer mattered that the leather of his boots was soaked through, for she was in his arms, her eyes focused only on him. Her brown irises were rimed in gold, and he was mesmerized by what he found deep within, an invitation to enter into her heart, her world. To become part of her, and he could not refuse, no more than he could not breathe.

When she licked her lips, he lowered his head to claim them. They were the softest, warmest, fullest lips he had ever tasted. He opened his mouth, covering the entirety of hers, and as he closed it, moving his lips over hers, he slid his tongue to the outer surface of her mouth. The smooth sensation was intoxicating, and Fitzwilliam Darcy never wanted to leave. He felt her lips move against his, and when they parted her tongue touched his. It was as if lightening struck and he clutched her to him, pressing every inch of her that he could onto his skin. She pulled back, taking in deep gulps of air. The release allowed him to do the same. Gaining some sense of where they were, he bent down and scooped her up in his arms, so that her bare feet now freely kicked the air around them. She squealed in delight as he moved them onto dry land walking to the large rock, where she had laid her garments.

She looked shyly at him, and said, "We must return soon, or we shall be missed."

"I do not care, Elizabeth. Do you?"

She looked at him, thoughtfully. "I do not know, Mr. Darcy."

"Mr. Darcy?" He came closer to her. "Surely we have moved beyond Mr. Darcy and your Grace, at least when we are alone together."

She remained silent while gathering her stockings. "Turn around, so I may reapply my garter."

"I think not, milady," he said with a rakish grin. "Allow me to assist you." He took the stocking from her hand, and before she knew what he was about, he slipped the rolled stocking over her toes. He held her ankle, his fingers caressing down to the arch of her foot. He traced the stocking as it rose up her leg, sensually riding higher and higher to her thigh. When he had run out of fabric, he held out a hand for her garter which she handed over, with a sweet huff. Placing her now stocking-clad foot on his thigh, he maneuvered the garter over her toes, repeating his earlier motions until the garter was in place, mid-thigh. Then he brought both hands up under her skirts to test the tension.

As he began the process with her other leg, he noted with great satisfaction that Elizabeth's breath was as labored as his own. Keeping his eye on her, he raised her skirt over her knee, and he bent to place a loving kiss there, and then licked her skin before covering it with silk. Her moan was music to his ears. When the second garter had been tested, he let his hands linger on her legs as he guided her skirts to fall back to her toes. He then looked up at her and said, "Now, I believe we are ready to return."

He gathered his things and went to fetch the horses, grazing nearby. Elizabeth took the time to collect herself so she could continue in control of her mount. When they returned to Netherfield, they were rewarded with Jane and Mr. Bingley sitting side-by-side, heads nearly touching, on a bench in the middle of the rose garden.

~ CHAPTER SEVEN ~

November 1811
Purvis Lodge, Hertfordshire

Conversation between Purvis Lodge and Netherfield continued on a nearly daily basis. It was obvious to Darcy that his friend was enamored of the eldest Bennet sister. This bothered him not, as it enabled him to remain in company with Elizabeth. He took every opportunity to be in her presence. When in her presence, he felt alive in a way previously unknown to him. He relished the time he could be near her, cherished the moments when he was alone with her, although it seemed to him after their frolic in the pond that she was reluctant in allowing such liberties.

With memories of these stolen moments dancing in his mind, Darcy moved Elizabeth off to a secluded path on one of their unofficial meetings.

"Your Grace, a moment of your time?" he asked, uncertainty evident in his manor and voice. She nodded, following his lead. "I received a letter from Georgiana," he noted Elizabeth's attention perking up. "She is..." he looked away, uncomfortable with his report. "She is... her mood is despondent." Elizabeth approached him, concern on her face.

"She is not ill?" Elizabeth asked, trying to rule out causes for the young woman's distress.

"She is in fine health, Elizabeth." Her name had escaped his lips before he could stop. It felt so good, too good to deny himself the simple pleasure of claiming such intimacy. Elizabeth felt his presence close to her, threatening to overwhelm her reserve. She had not felt this vulnerable since Rafael had asked for her hand. Struggling to calm her good sense, she focused on Georgiana.

"If it is not her health, how may I help?" she avoided calling him by name, unwilling to participate in the intimacy, but loathe to return to a more formal address.

He looked at her intently, 'Say you will come live with me and be my love,' he thought, but said, "I was hoping you might invite her to visit. Her stay with you and Dame Agatha made her the happiest I have seen her... in an age."

"Of course. She is always welcome, surely you know that."

"I believe at the moment, she has forgotten..."

"Of course. Shall I write to her? We return to London for the holidays." Darcy's eyes filled with hope.

"May I invite you and your party to dine at Darcy House one evening? And perhaps an evening at the theater, or opera?" 'Or both,' he thought.

"And perhaps *you* should wait to hear how large my intended party will be, Mr. Darcy, before issuing your invitation." She laughed and Darcy's heart felt light and free. "My entire family will be joining Agatha and myself, and the boys of course. Perhaps dinner *en famille,* and I will defer on the theater until," her eyes looked into his and she was lost. "Until," she breathed, heavily, "until it is just Jane and I?"

He smiled in pleasure witnessing her discomposure. "As you wish, your Grace. May I return later this afternoon, or tomorrow to retrieve your letter to my sister?" He stepped closer, his arm encircling her waist as he pulled her to him. "Elizabeth," his lips claimed hers, and she responded, her arms sliding up his chest till she could run her fingers through the curls on the back of his neck.

"Oh, William," she whispered, and Darcy felt heaven open, allowing him a glimpse of paradise. But it was over too quickly. Elizabeth pulled back mortified at the betrayal of her desire. "Mr. Darcy, I… I know not what overcame me."

"I do, milady." He was crushed by her words. "When, Elizabeth, when will you allow your feelings their due? When?"

"It is too soon!"

"Rafael," he shouted before stopping himself. Taking a moment to calm his jealousy, Darcy began again. "He is gone, Elizabeth… nearly two years. Life is for the living. I do not ask that you abandon his memory, I only wish to know if there is room in your heart… for me."

She looked at him with fear. His anger melted, and he took her hand gently to his lips. "Only tell me there is hope, and we will work this out between us. My feelings for you, Elizabeth, are powerful. But I will hold them… in… until you are ready to receive me."

She attempted to take back her hand, but he held it firm. Looking into his eyes, she felt completely vulnerable. There was no hiding, she knew this. What she did not know was whether or not she had the strength to endure the fire yet again. When she looked at him, though, she knew, she would find the way, somehow, to love again.

She nodded and he covered her hand with his free one. He brought both back to his mouth, closing his eyes only when his parted lips touched the smooth skin of the back of her palm. She took his hands, moving to reveal his skin before bestowing a kiss to his knuckles. He gasped and she smiled. He then offered her his arm, and they went to find Bingley and Miss Bennet.

A few days later, Darcy found himself staring out the window of his room, his thoughts focused on the Duchess. There were moments when he was sure of her feelings for him, but in honesty he was certain of nothing. There were times when her eyes found him, and he shivered, just before his blood caught fire forcing him to recover at a windowsill, where his discomposure was less noticeable. Then, he would say or do something that set her off and she would withdraw her favor. Most times it was when, in conversation with Caroline, he would make a comment about the inferiority of the local society, or the need to maintain the distinction of rank. Then, he would look up finding her eyes flashing, her lips pursed in almost a pout ready to launch a verbal assault upon him so swift and accurate that if they were fencing, he was sure he would be dead.

Never in his eight and twenty years had he experienced such a tumult of emotions. One moment he was in full command of his faculties, the next he was unsure of the ground under his feet. He felt vulnerable and confused and he did not like it one bit. He found courage and an emotional salve in the brandy he shared after dinner with Bingley and Hurst, and found a modicum of comfort in the regularity and predictability inherent in the conversation of the Netherfield ladies.

~

As the gentlemen rode up the drive to Purvis Lodge, Elizabeth stood before him, her cheeks flushed from the exercise of walking with Jane. Her eyes were bright and sparkling. The gentlemen had, again, finished their morning ride of delivering invitations to the upcoming ball, with visit to their neighboring estate.

"Mr. Darcy! How good to see you, and you Mr. Bingley, again." Bingley had the good grace to blush at Elizabeth's tease.

After kissing her raised hand, Darcy began, "Thank you, your Grace. As we are about the business of a ball, I would ask for the first set, if I may?" He had not meant to blurt it out quite like that, but he could wait no longer.

"You may, Mr. Darcy. That is if I ever receive my invitation to this grand spectacle." She looked with wide-eyed innocence at Mr. Bingley, who blushed again. Darcy cleared his throat and looked to his friend.

"Yes, that is what we are at present… engaged in… that is, we are distributing the invitations to my ball," Charles stammered.

"Ah, well, as soon as I have mine in hand, sir, I will give you your answer."

Darcy glared at his friend.

"Your Grace," Bingley began, bringing Jane and himself closer to Elizabeth and her partner. "It seems, I have yet again forgotten yours, and that for the Bennets. I will have to return to properly deliver it … perhaps tomorrow?" Both he and Jane blushed, while Elizabeth nearly lost her composure laughing. She looked up at Darcy who caught her mirth hiding his own behind a cough.

"Well, you may wish to visit my parents first, Mr. Bingley, as *I* have the good fortune of having Jane with me for the rest of the week." Her eyes twinkled, and it was all Darcy could do to keep from sweeping her in his arms and absconding with her to the woods.

~

Elizabeth looked in on her father, alone in his study. Since his illness, he had opted to remain downstairs near his beloved books. He still nourished the hope he would eventually walk unaided, and felt eliminating the stairs may hasten that miracle.

She found him asleep, his book magnifying the rise and fall of his chest. Elizabeth entered, quietly, gently removing the tome, noting her father seemed fixated on Shakespeare's *The Tempest* more often than not. After wiping the wisps of hair teasing his brow, Elizabeth sat on the chair nearby. 'How frail he appears,' she thought, her hands grasping the leather volume now lovingly held in her hand. 'When did he become so old?' The fluttering of his eyes alerted Elizabeth to his wakening.

"Good morning, my dear," he sputtered. "How wonderful to find you the first vision of my day."

She smiled happily recalling mornings of their past when they would walk the meadows to greet dawn's first light from Oakum Mount. She sighed realizing they would never enjoy such indulgences again. "How are you this morning, Pappa?"

"Well, now that you are here, Lizzy."

Again she smiled and stretched her hand to clasp his. His eyes, undaunted by the limits of his body, bore into her asking the source of her distress.

"Come, my dear, tell me what troubles you." She looked away. "Now Elizabeth, you were never any good at hiding... at least not from me." He looked at her, piecing together what he had heard while Mrs. Bennet,

Lydia and Kitty gossiped thinking he slept. "Could it be the Netherfield party that preys upon your equanimity?" Her gasp alerted him to his accuracy. "Has this Mr. Darcy upset you?" She smiled half-heartedly.

"Not in the manner you think, sir. It is just... I feel... confused... when he is near." Noting the concerned look on her father's face, she quickly added, "He is always the gentleman, Papa, it is only I feel in danger... of... of loving him, and am frightened to do so."

"Frightened, Elizabeth? You? The most fearless person I know?"

"Indeed, Father. *He* is very intense, not so easy a man as... Rafael was so open, so easy to be with. He just took my love and gave his so easily. There was never any doubt or moment when I felt I would lose myself." She had abruptly risen out of her chair and now paced in front of the window. Her father unable to follow her movements closed his eyes and listened to all her voice and words would reveal.

"There are times... when he looks at me... that I feel I will lose my very soul..." and she added very quietly, but not quietly enough, "... willingly."

Mr. Bennet made a great effort to turn to be able to catch the end of a look on his daughter's face that completed the picture her voice had sketched. "Elizabeth..." he called. She returned to him, kneeling by the makeshift bed upon which he lay. "Emotion of such strength holds great potential... for bliss or destruction. Bliss if you welcome it into your life, heedless yet cognizant of the power it holds over you. To embrace such emotion is the challenge of our lifetimes and we must... clasp onto it. To let it pass by may appear to be the easy way, but it will double back and kick you down, stomp your spirit into the dirt. Regret turns into bitterness and indifference, my darling. And it would break my heart if the sins of this father come to rest upon you, my beloved child."

Thomas Bennet held on to his daughter's hand even as she would pull away, forcing her by the strength of his undiminished gaze, to look upon him, full in the eye. What she found there was full understanding and an unspoken plea to heed his advice. While fearful at first, she clung to him, allowing the confidence of his soul to comfort her. Elizabeth felt her heart fill and her tears fall until they heard the bustle outside as the door opened and Mrs. Bennet and Mrs. Hill hurried in.

When Elizabeth, Agatha and Jane Bennet entered the hall, they were greeted by Charles and Caroline Bingley, along with Louisa and Stephen Hurst. Mr. Bingley was effusive in his joy at their arrival, amusing Agatha tremendously. Netherfield was resplendent in the decorations Miss Bingley had orchestrated. The Bennet sisters shone in a rare type of silk. Jane wore ivory with a blush of blue. She had sapphires around her neck and dangling from her ears. Mr. Bingley caught by the duties of a good host, was forced to relinquish Miss Bennet's hand until the first set. Elizabeth's gown shimmered rose when the light hit it, and she was adorned with the rubies Rafael had first gifted her.

As the ladies made their way to the main hall, Louisa's attention was drawn by her sister's commentary. "Honestly, you would think the wench had never been to London! And people think she is the epitome of taste! I long to return to London and let loose word of her wild appearance. Just wait till Lady Jervis hears about that plain gown. And her hair! An unrulier mass of curls I have never seen. Oh, yes, one word whispered in Lady Megstan's ear and that will be the end of her!"

Louisa had listened to her sister's barrage in between greeting their guests. She also noted Mr. Darcy watching, his eyes narrowed in suspicion. She smiled at him, trying to convey by her look that she was helpless to stop Caroline's mutterings without causing a scene.

The musicians finally indicated the beginning of the dance. Darcy went in search of Elizabeth. He passed Miss Bingley, who stood positioning herself for his hand for the first set. As he passed by, something in Miss Bingley shattered. She sent daggers down his back until he bowed before Elizabeth. Seeing her position at his side taken, she transferred her venom to her rival.

Darcy bowed gratefully, eager to feast his gaze upon Elizabeth. She bowed in curtsey, and when he took her hand, the world fell away. Only they existed, partnered, while the music moved them about. They walked to the head of the line, standing behind Bingley and the eldest Bennet sister. They bowed as the dance required. Darcy felt he was floating as she came toward him, circling him, her curls bouncing enticingly. Thoughts of where he would wish those curls to fall ran through his mind, and his breathing became shallow, his desire banking into a raging fire. In an attempt to regain his composure, he forced himself to look away from her beauty and the peace he found when he found himself gazing into her eyes.

Elizabeth felt her pulse race the moment Darcy touched her to lead her to the dance. His hand upon hers, even through the combined layers of their gloves, warmed her. Her heart, her body responded, wanting more of whatever he was doing to her. 'It has been so long,' she thought, 'since anyone has touched me so. And yet it is not yet two years since Rafael…'

He could see the distress on her features, could read it in her fine eyes. "Elizabeth, are you well?" he asked, desirous to rid her of her distress, even if it was created by his presence, though 'I pray that is not the case.'

"I am well, sir. Only confused."

He caught his breath unable to speak. "May I ask, what is it that confuses you, madam?"

"You, sir. You and the feelings you bring forth in me."

The heat that enveloped Darcy colored his cheeks and hers. He looked deeply into her eyes, but could not say another word. He needed to focus on the steps, as his mind was running away with him, to how quickly he could run away with her.

∾

The remainder of the ball was awhirl as Elizabeth danced with many of the men she had shared childhood with. In the back of her awareness she felt Darcy watching her. He was always there in the periphery, and nary three paces away lurked Caroline Bingley. While dancing she blocked out the dark cloud, but in between, while awaiting a glass of champagne, or sitting near a breeze, she could feel those cold eyes upon her. She shivered.

Caroline approached the Duchess, implementing her well rehearsed attack.

"Duchess, how unusual to see *you* sitting while the music still plays," Caroline tried to keep her voice light, and pleasing.

Elizabeth eyed her warily. She only nodded. Caroline continued. "You are so very popular, your Grace. All these men are practically embarrassing themselves to get near their prize."

"These are men… are people I have known all my life, Miss Bingley. This is the first time I have been in society since… I am sure they only wish to make my re-entry to society as pleasant as possible."

"Indeed! How solicitous. Still…" letting her eye roam she noted that Darcy had taken up his position nearby. "To be the center of so much *male* attention, you must be thrilled."

Elizabeth rose, disgusted by the tone of the conversation. "They are my friends, Miss Bingley, and nothing more. I look at them as Mr. Darcy looks at *you*. As an acquaintance, that is all." Elizabeth left the viper's den as Mr. Darcy came to claim her for his next set. Miss Bingley watched them move to the floor. She sat stewing. 'Oh, my dear Lady Eliza, you may see them as such, but that hardly signifies. It matters more, oh, so much more how others see them ...'

~

Caroline was at table when the members of the Netherfield party meandered into the breakfast room the morning after the ball. "Charles, what a success this evening has been..."

"I owe you a great deal, Caro, the results were well worth your effort."

She bowed her head in recognition of his praise.

"Yes, Miss Bingley, an unqualified success," added Darcy feeling it necessary to compliment his hostess.

"Thank you, Mr. Darcy. I must say, to entertain not one but two peers is quite an accomplishment, and it was evident that at the very least the Duchess of Gainsbridge enjoyed herself last evening." From the corner of her eye, she watched her words find their mark. He bristled at her next utterance. "Yes, Lady Elizabeth had hardly a moment to herself all evening! The belle of the ball, I am sure. Her name on the lips of all the gentlemen..."

Caroline took a sip of her now cold coffee.

"Indeed." Darcy turned away from the harridan and said to his friend, "Bingley, what say you to a ride out this morning? Something to clear the mind?"

"Excellent idea, Darcy. I will have our horses saddled."

Caroline watched as the men conversed about their mounts, carefully observing the faraway looks in their eyes.

'Enjoy your little fantasies, gentlemen. When I am done with you, those dreams will reside where they belong, in the ash heap.' "If you will excuse me, I believe I have letters to write."

Caroline retired for the afternoon writing her friend Lady Bledsole, a woman with whom she shared her greatest pleasure, the spreading of gossip.

~

London
February, 1812

The Gainsbridges had been in London for almost three weeks, settling into a comfortable pattern of entertaining two toddling boys as well as maintaining a social calendar. Due to Mr. Bennet's continued convalescence, not even Jane returned to London with their entourage. Mrs. Bates, nurse to Rafael and Ian, had the lads firmly in line with morning playtime in the nursery and a mid-morning walk. Then they would eat with their mother and great aunt, nap and have a late afternoon romp. To their extreme delight, their mother, *Aunt* Georgie and sometimes Great Aunt Agatha would often accompany Mrs. Bates on their outings, scattering bread crumbs for the ducks and swans, or rolling snowballs into odd shapes to be knocked down at will. It was a pattern they kept to as Mrs. Bates firmly believed that well ordered, secure children thrived on routine.

However, routines are easy to discern, especially when one's intent is to malign.

~

Wydom House,London
March, 1812

Jane came to Wyndom House to help her sister endure the coming season. Both Elizabeth and Agatha had written imploring her to come. She missed Elizabeth and the boys, but was hesitant to leave Longbourn. Even with the capable steward Elizabeth had hired, she felt it was her duty to care for their family. And yet, it had been before Christmas that she had last seen Charles Bingley, and she was curious as to his intentions. Elizabeth had written that he asked after '*our dear Miss Bennet*' when she encountered him at the fashionable events Agatha dragged her to, or when Mr. Darcy came to tea. One of his business interests had ships taken by the French, and Bingley's presence was needed to calm the fears of his partners and investors. And with Jane tied to Longbourn, there was not much she was able to do to further the match. Although spring planting was approaching, it was Agatha's last letter that convinced Jane to travel to London.

It was with hope and trepidation that she greeted the fine stone façade of Wyndom House. The luxurious Gainsbridge coach made the ride comfortable, and was for the most part, uneventful. Her measurements had been sent to Elizabeth's modiste, so there were certain to be fine gowns waiting, and many engagements to face. Yet her heart was troubled. Agatha's letters spoke of Elizabeth's unease, her sense that something was not right. Her grief had not seemed to dissipate. Agatha was not sure of the cause, but something troubled her niece, and she was counting on Jane to ferret it out.

Dame Agatha forced Elizabeth and Jane to attend more balls and dinners than Elizabeth had the stomach for, but to disoblige them from notions of despair, she capitulated. At every engagement there were many willing to dance and occupy her every moment, should she so desire. And there were more than enough to satisfy her more… intimate desires, should she wish. While out in society, Elizabeth made sure to remain near Agatha's side, or Jane's or Agatha's cousin Edwin, Lord Aubrey.

Darcy found his social calendar full as was his custom, but for this season he was eager, not reticent. He attended more balls in one month than he had the last three years. There was one reason and one reason only: Elizabeth. She was dazzling and enticing and slowly, patiently, he plied his course, courting her surreptitiously. He was at her side as often as possible, escorting her,

Jane and Dame Agatha to balls, dinners, and the theater as often as he could manage. She smiled at him, laughed at and with him, and engaged him in such lively discussion, his soul was thrilled.

Dark moments came when some young reprobate tried to impose himself on her. 'I never knew so many rakes inhabited London,' he thought with disdain. 'How can she bear it?' he glared as yet another claimed her for a dance. While she swirled about in the arms of another man, Darcy kept his eyes upon her graceful form. His single minded focus left him vulnerable to the approaching Randall Scott.

"Darcy, old man. How are you?"

Darcy winced at the outstretched hand, loathe to tear his eyes away from Elizabeth. Following his gaze, Scott said with appreciation. "Ah, the lovely widow Gainsbridge." Seeing his Cambridge friend stiffen, he added. "You must admit, Lady Gainsbridge is both a treasure to be *gained*, and a bridge to be *surmounted*."

Darcy summoned every once of self-restraint to avoid strangling his university acquaintance. Seeing Darcy's temple throb, Scott smiled and patted him on the arm. "Shall I warn off the others?"

Darcy growled.

"Or perhaps let it all play itself out. It has been quite a long time since a true cock fight has captivated the halls of London society."

Darcy stepped closer, saying with menace in his voice. "If I hear another word about the Duchess, anything that blemishes her reputation you or any of your *followers* shall have me to answer to, Scott. Do I make myself clear?"

"Perfectly, Darcy." Scott said brushing off the front of his evening jacket as if something unpleasant had landed there. "But," he warned with a hint of menace of his own. "You shall not be the only one sniffing about Gainsbridge's door."

Recalling Rafael's heartfelt plea to spare Elizabeth being hounded by every man with a pulse for either her beauty or her wealth, Darcy scowled again, and turned as Scott walked away. Desperately, he sought out Elizabeth and when she turned around her partner, his eyes locked onto hers. Seeing her eyes brighten, he smiled, and her response was brilliant. He felt his heart momentarily stop, then begin again, pounding at twice its normal rate. As her partner reclaimed her hand, she rolled her eyes, and Darcy's neighbors heard the most unusual sound, that of Fitzwilliam Darcy chuckling out loud, and in public. Tongues were atwitter and gossip streamed across the hall, like the wind rippling through a meadow of tall grass.

When the gossip reached the ears of Caroline Bingley three days later, she was enraged.

"How dare he?" she screamed when safely encased in her chambers after taking tea with Miss Simpson. "After all this time, to be so... enamored with that... that social pariah!" She prowled the length of her room, her fists clenching nervously. She suddenly stopped in the midst of her room. 'I will fix that little upstart. Pemberley is mine! And no country miss, duchess or not, will take what belongs to Caroline Darcy!'

The next week Darcy received an express informing him of fire that had consumed one of his tenant's homes. Dispatching Georgiana to Wyndom House, he headed north. Claiming her duty as guardian, Elizabeth begged off the social obligations Agatha had committed her to. They had dinner with the Fitzwilliams, Lord Aubrey, the Gardiners and an occasional evening concert or theatrical performance.

One such theatrical evening with Lord Aubrey and Dame Agatha in attendance, their serenity was disturbed by a knock on the door.

"Enter," Lord Aubrey called out.

"Pardon the interruption," a young man began, taking in the opulence through large, doe-like eyes. "But I could hardly let the opportunity slip through my fingers to come and greet you." Lord Aubrey looked at the young man not yet twenty, searching his face for recognition. The man saw his elder's confusion and stepped in. "Forgive me, Lord Aubrey, it has been a few years since we last met. I am Robert Danvers."

"Danvers! My God, man, you are right, it has been an age!" Everyone in the box relaxed at Aubrey's enthusiasm. "How are you, lad? And your parents?" The boy blushed and Dame Agatha coughed. "Oh, forgive me, where are my manners? Lord Danvers, may I introduce my cousin, Agatha Pembroke, the Duchess of Leicester, Elizabeth Gainsbridge Duchess of Deronshire,

Mr. and Mrs. Edward Gardiner, Miss Jane Bennet and Miss Georgiana Darcy."

Four pairs of eyes locked on to the introduction as the young lord bowed to each, but addressed only the youngest member of their party.

"A true pleasure, Miss Darcy."

"Thank you, Lord Danvers."

"Danvers, my boy, will you join us for the rest of the evening?"

The young man nodded and took the seat between Elizabeth and Georgiana.

Across the theater in a rented box, Caroline smiled as she took in the details through her opera glasses.

Elizabeth walked a pace behind Miss Bates and the boys. She was weary, her nights interrupted by disturbing dreams that began pleasant enough, with agreeable company, most often Mr. Darcy paying her particular attention. Then, as their conversation became more intimate, without fail, a note would appear, its message always the same, *'I know how weak you truly are. Soon all you cherish will be mine. You and all you love will be crushed.'* She woke, as she had for the weeks these nightmares had haunted her, in a cold sweat.

When the notes did in fact begin to appear, hand delivered by varying street urchins, her panic kept her from enough slumber to even dream. After having a footman accompany Mrs. Bates and her children, she arranged to have the urchins followed but inevitably they would evade their shadow, escaping into the bowels of London.

~

Darcy returned to London nearly a month after learning of the fire at Pemberley. His thoughts focused exclusively on Elizabeth, to see her, claim her. Reaching the outskirts of town, he noted how the gentle rain that dogged him for the last half an hour was devolving into a fierce storm. Looking to the skies he cursed the forces that brought the torrent, drowning his hopes of seeing Elizabeth. The following morning, his attention was deterred by a contract sent over by his solicitor. After a difficult two hours reviewing the papers, he heard a knock upon his door.

"Enter," he called out, sitting up straight in his chair. Looking up, he saw his butler, Hastings, standing their waiting for his acknowledgment. "Yes, what is it?"

"Mr. Bingley, sir." Seeing the confusion of his employer, the man continued. "He and his sisters have come to call, sir."

'How could they know I am in London? I arrived only last evening!.' Shaking his head, he addressed his man. "Very well. I shall be with them shortly. Thank you, Hastings."

"Very good, sir."

Emerging from his study his mind still pondering how the Bingleys could know of his return, Darcy steeled himself to endure tea with Miss Bingley, her sister and their brother. Facing his fate, he headed down the hall to join his guests. Hearing his booted step in the hall, Miss Bingley expertly directed the conversation to Lord Danvers.

"I have *heard*, that Lord Danvers has become a frequent caller upon Wyndom House."

Both Louisa and Charles looked at her strangely, as they had been talking about the Hursts's new carriage.

Caroline continued, her voice louder, carrying further down the hall. "How lovely for the Duchess, to have such a handsome young... admirer... at her beck and call."

"Miss Bingley, Mrs. Hurst, Bingley! How... pleasant to see you again," Darcy interrupted.

Mrs. Hurst watched as Caroline wove her web.

"Oh, Mr. Darcy. We were just speaking of the Duchess Gainsbridge and the attention Lord Danvers seems to bestow upon her," Caroline simpered.

Darcy looked as if he had been slapped.

"I was unaware they were acquainted," his tone was clipped.

"I believe Lord Aubrey introduced them," Charles offered, trying to stem the growing ire in his friend. "I have met him at Wyndom House on occasion. He is a very pleasant gentleman."

"Indeed." Wishing to change the subject, Mrs. Hurst mentioned a promising new composer she had heard of, and they spoke of music until the Bingleys left for another appointment.

~

Darcy's luck had not improved. He had managed to see Elizabeth briefly, when he returned Georgiana back to Darcy House. The boys were in ill temper and Elizabeth was preoccupied with calming them, so a private audience was postponed. He had attended all social events he thought she might attend, but she was no where to be seen. The next week, when he was loosing patience and hope of seeing her, he found himself at a dinner party accompanied by Mr. and Mrs. Hurst and their sister, Caroline.

"I had the most charming conversation the other day, Mr. Darcy," purred Caroline Bingley as she slipped onto the sofa next to the handsome man. The gentleman stiffened and imperceptively shifted his frame turning away from her insincere smile.

Noting his reluctance, she added the ingredient she knew would entice his attention. "Yes," she drawled. "The other day, Miss Bennet accompanied Louisa and I to tea..." Caroline waited as Darcy reacted exactly as she had expected, snapping to attention. Smiling inwardly at the ease of her machinations she continued. "She mentioned how *active* her home-away-from-home is at the moment." Darcy's distress warmed Caroline's heart as she pressed forward, leaning into her companion's strong arm. "Such a distraction while those young children languish in their sick beds. So many visitors, *gentlemen* callers coming at all hours of the day..." Caroline stirred the tea in front of her watching the liquid churn as she moved the ornate silver spoon. "One would think with her reputation," Caroline hesitated, "as such a *fine* mother that she would limit the traffic to-and-from her home." Sighing to cover her delight Caroline added, "I suppose there is no curbing some appetites, is there?" The thin woman smiled wickedly, thanking her lucky stars that she had met Jane and her Aunt Gardiner in a rather fashionable tea shop and listened to their tedious tales of the young Gardiners and their sniffling and coughing, and how they interfered with Mr. Gardiner who's office was being repaired due to a leaky roof. Jane had mentioned the chaos of the office clerks coming and going, while Mr. Gardiner's attempted to complete a particularly important piece of business.

"She....she receives visitors?" Darcy asked despite every fiber of his mind screamed to disengage from this conversation.

"Oh, yes. My brother, poor fool, visits daily."

Darcy waited a long and unending day before storming over to Wyndom House. When the door opened he was led to Agatha in the parlor. "Where is she?"

"Darcy? What on Earth do you mean coming here in this state? Is it your intent to frighten us? I will not allow you to upset her. She is..."

"Where is she? He snarled, an agitated hand running through his uncombed hair.

"Pull yourself together, man! You look a fright!"

Taken aback, Darcy stopped and shot an inquiring look in a mirror. Shocked, he patted down his hair and his jacket. The moment gave him the chance to calm his nerves which had been whipped into a frenzy of lurid imaginings of the kisses and embraces Elizabeth had gifted him being scattered among others. "Why does she keep me away?"

"Keep you? What are you talking about?"

Helplessly he looked to her. "Wyndom House has been closed…"

"To visitors, yes. Ian and Rafe have suffered with a fever and Elisabeth wished to contain it."

"But Bingley…"

Agatha laughed ignorant of the tempest brewing in Darcy's heart. "I believe Mr. Bingley continues to court Miss Bennet at the Gardiner's home, in Cheapside."

Darcy looked abashed. "Then there have been no callers here?"

"No social calls for days." Agatha shook her head. "You are the first, Darcy."

The opening of the study door interrupted their conversations as both watched in varying degrees of concern as Elizabeth and an unknown man emerged. Before noting the attention they collected, the man said in a soft, assuring voice, "Fear not, your Grace, I shall be the soul of discretion…" The sound of boot steps approaching stopped them and he protectively stepped in front of Elizabeth.

"Elizabeth!" Darcy called as his excitement at seeing her shattered as the unknown interloper blocked his view, protecting the Duchess as Darcy felt was his right. Casting a withering glace at both Elizabeth and Agatha he growled. "I see, no social visitors, but a constant stream of callers. *Gentlemen* callers." Straightening his spine, he added. "Well, I will not trespass on your hospitality again." And he walked away, leaving the astounded trio in his wake.

~ CHAPTER EIGHT ~

May, 1812
London

Darcy found himself more in the company of Bingley and his sisters than with Elizabeth. Georgiana continued to visit Wyndom House, enjoying the sisterly camaraderie she felt there. Every evening when she would return to Darcy House, Georgiana would torture her brother with stories of how Elizabeth was constantly with her sons, tending to their stuffy noses, reading them stories trying to enliven their sick room. He smiled at her tender care, and told Georgiana of stories their parents would recite when he was a young boy. He knew she would offer them to Elizabeth so she could entertain the children. When a letter was delivered to him from Wyndom House Darcy was beside himself, entertaining his lifelong butler with flustered behavior. His man smiled seeing his taciturn employer bluster about, nearly knocking over the chair as he made his way to his study, the lavender scent of the letter wafting down the hall. Darcy's fingers trembled as they caressed the fine weave of the parchment. They traced her initials imposed upon the Gainsbridge seal. He ran his finger beneath the lip of the paper until it met with the resistance of the wax. He ran his finger back to the edge, and then, with a sudden movement the seal was broken, its content revealed.

Mr. Darcy,

Please forgive the impropriety of receiving this letter, but your last story of the little boy-pirate delighted Ian immensely. Now Rafael demands his own tale and not having much experience with his Majesty's navy, I implore you to send a sequel. Perhaps this one you could deliver in person. Your audience awaits you.

With warm regards,
Elizabeth Gainsbridge

His relief was profound. Since his outburst, he had missed her immensely. More often than not he would reread the poems, the books they had discussed, or attend the exhibits of artists she had mentioned a preference for. He sought her in the printed word, or the work of art on the gallery wall. This little piece of paper he held in his hand liberated his heart. She had acknowledged his gift, the stories of his childhood, stories he hoped to share with his children, her children, their children. And that she asked for him to come and share these bits of himself with her sons filled his chest with warmth, and he smiled. Armed with the knowledge she desired his company, he found he could manage another evening with the Bingley siblings and their gossip.

Darcy found himself drawing on Elizabeth's letter later that evening as he made his way toward his box with the Bingleys and Hursts. Lord Danvers approached, inquiring after Miss Bennet, Miss Darcy and of course, the Duchess Gainsbridge. Darcy's attention was acutely focused on the young man when Miss Bingley asked, "Lord Danvers, how did you find the Duchess when last you saw her?"

Taken aback by the tone more than the words, Danvers observed the woman before him. "Her Grace is as always, perfection." Darcy felt his heart shudder. The lad continued, as Caroline watched Darcy with the keen eyes of a hawk. "No matter what, she..." reconsidering his line of thought, he simply said, "astounds those fortunate enough to call her friend."

"Indeed," purred Caroline looking up at the clenched jaw of her tall, dark companion.

Darcy finally contributed to the conversation, his voice clipped, cold. "Have you known her Grace long?" Darcy noted that the young man was comely, and his frame substantial. In many ways he reminded Darcy of a younger version of himself, and he bristled.

"No, only in the last few months, since her return to town. Lord Aubrey introduced us one evening at the theater."

"Ah," he said, scanning his memory for information on that evening. Georgiana had spoken about that night, how delightful were the performers, how attentive the visitors to Lord Aubrey's box. How fortunate she felt to have Elizabeth to guide her, as, she thought, would an older sister.

"I was fortunate to meet your sister, then, as well, sir. Everything a lovely young lady should be..." Danvers smiled at the recollection, but Darcy just scowled.

Darcy dismissed the notion that Danvers could be interested in his sister, for while it would be convenient, no one compared to Elizabeth, especially a girl who was not even out in society. Darcy was unable to confide his fears in Bingley, who was so absorbed in his romance with Miss Jane Bennet to notice the undercurrents of others swirling around him. 'No, better to soldier on, and try and resolve this one way or another.'

"Well, if you will excuse me, my friends await upstairs. It has been a pleasure seeing you again, Mr. Bingley. Miss Bingley, Mrs. Hurst, Mr. Hurst, Mr. Darcy." Danvers bowed to all before departing.

Taking her sister by the elbow, Caroline began ascending the stairs herself, speaking in a clear and audible whisper, "So, that is Lord Danvers," she looked back at the gentlemen following her and her sister. "Such a fine young man, what a coup for him to have such access to Wyndom House. One can only imagine how her *Grace* employs her pert tongue on such a handsome young man?" They twittered as Darcy, Bingley and Hurst kept pace a few steps behind them.

~

Elizabeth sat with her sister, Jane, in her private parlor when Mrs. Bates requested an interview. Elizabeth was about to send her away, but the woman's distress wiped those thoughts from her mind.

"Your Grace, please, forgive the interruption..."

"No, no, Mrs. Bates, what is it?" Elizabeth jumped out of her seat bringing the older woman to come and sit with them, by the fire. "Are you well? The boys?" Panic was evident in her eyes.

"The wee ones are fine." With that Elizabeth pulled back, her eyes like ice. Mrs. Bates looked to Jane, and then back to her. Elizabeth nodded.

"You may speak freely before my sister, Mrs. Bates. Now, tell me this instant what has frightened you so."

Looking down at her hands, Mrs. Bates took a breath before looking Elizabeth straight in the eyes, sighing. "It was as I told you, before." She maintained direct eye contact. "I cannot shake this feeling that someone watches while their Graces are out in the park."

"Start from the beginning, Mrs. Bates. You took the boys nearly an hour ago, correct?" their mother inquired.

"Yes, as is our habit. We left at 3:00 to walk by the ponds, and feed the ducks. Lord Ian likes his punctuality. Feels the birds depend on him." Despite the concern in the room, all three women let their lips twitch at the fastidious Ian imperiously commanding his nurse to keep to her schedule.

"Go on..." Elizabeth quelled the laugh she longed to release.

"We arrived at the pond, and the birds were waiting for us. Rafael dropped his bag, and as I bent to pick it up, I turned and felt someone was... close by."

"Certainly there were other people in the park, Mrs. Bates," offered Jane trying to make some sense of the woman's ramblings.

"No, ma'am, there was not. I called out, as we were nearby a little copse of trees. No one answered, and I stood watch for quite a while, keeping the boys in my line of sight all the while. When Rafael called to me, I turned, and moments later, I swear to you, your Grace," here Mrs. Bates leaned forward to Elizabeth. "I swear I heard someone move about in the trees. I called the boys to me, and without too much of a fuss, went near where there were people milling about, until I could gather my wits and return home."

Elizabeth sat still, thinking about all Mrs. Bates had said. Reaching a conclusion, she turned to the woman, "Mrs. Bates. When you next take the boys out, please ask Mr. Smothers to have one of the footmen accompany you." She was about to speak, but looking at Jane, held her tongue.

"Thank you, ma'am," said the older woman with relief. She rose and curtsied to her employer and her sister, then left the room.

"Mrs. Bates?" called out Elizabeth.

"Yes, your Grace?"

"Why do you not go and see Mrs. Reardon, and take a nice cup of tea, and perhaps a sherry?"

"Thank you, ma'am." Mrs. Bates bobbed her head, smiled and closed the door.

~

Darcy could not stay away from Elizabeth, taking exceptional pains to be present at the events he hoped she would attend. His heart warred with his reason; she had asked for time and while he struggled with it, he could accept this demand with some semblance of equanimity. But he could not accept her turning to another for comfort. While he yearned to see her, even in the presence of others, there never seemed to be a moment when he found her alone. A constant cadre of men surrounded her, hovering about like jackals hungering for a taste of her. To make matters worse, whenever Darcy would accompany Georgiana to Wyndom House, Danvers was always there, waiting.

Towards the end of the season, a mutual friend of Darcy and Rafael, Horace Esterbrook hosted a ball in honor of his wife's gifting him a son and heir. Darcy had arrived earlier than his habit, hoping to snatch a moment of Elizabeth's time. After enduring the mindless prattle of the matrons and their daughters angling for his interest, he was rewarded with one of the most breathtaking sights he had ever seen. There, gliding down the steps was Elizabeth on the arm of Lord Aubrey. On the gentleman's other arm stood Dame Agatha, reminding Darcy that Aubrey was one of Agatha's remaining relations. However, Darcy was not willing to give her companions any more thought and he refocused his attention on Elizabeth's graceful figure as she arrived on the main floor of the great hall. Before he knew what his feet were doing, he found himself bowing before her, and when he lifted his eyes, his heart cried out for mercy.

"Your Grace," he said on his second attempt to speak. He blushed, and when he looked into her eyes, his gasped at the merriment and absolution he found there.

"Mr. Darcy," she said, her voice sounding suspiciously breathless.

"You are radiant this evening." He said after clearing the emotion from his throat.

She blushed and murmured her "Thank you. You look very well, yourself."

It was his turn to blush and seeing a smile light her eyes, he offered his arm. Feeling her hand on his muscle sent a shiver of excitement through his body and, leading her to the side of the room he spoke. "Is it too much to ask, are you, would you dance the first with me?"

'Yes, sir. I would be honored."

Darcy was unaccustomed to the joy that rushed over him at her reply, and he smiled. Silently he led them to a less populated alcove where he hoped they could speak. "Lady Elizabeth, I fear I must apologize for my outburst the other day."

He felt her eyes examining him, felt her hesitation. "Oh," was her hushed reply. "Very well. I accept your apology, sir."

"Sir?" he looked at her, his eyes questioning her formality. He saw her eyes had become guarded. 'She hides something from me.' A fire burned in his breast, one whose flames were unrelenting and burned cold. 'Yet she holds her gaze. No, she is not one to back down. My God, what a woman.' "May I be so bold as to ask, who was that gentleman?"

"That, sir, is none of your concern."

"No?" he asked, menace creeping into his voice? "As I understood it, your husband, the Duke, requested of me that I make it my concern. Are you so careless with his regard?"

Darcy stared at her defiance extracting a perverse pleasure in exciting her ire. She stepped closer to him and his heart beat faster.

"I treasure each and every word my husband ever spoke to me, sir. Do not disparage my regard for him. Not now, or ever!"

The music beckoned, and Darcy made to lead them to the floor. Elizabeth stood her ground, unwilling to take his arm. "My lady?" he asked, marveling at her anew. She hesitated another moment before taking his arm, it seemed to him, reluctantly. Taking their place on the line, Darcy watched her, noting with concern and a growing sense of defeat her resistance growing. 'Perhaps such strident measures will not work in this instance,' he thought, shuddering when she lifted her eyes. Instead of the lively merriment she normally showed him, her eyes were formal, polite, cold.

~

At every other turn Caroline Bingley seemed to be waiting for Darcy, mentioning the latest gossip remarking on Elizabeth Gainsbridge's being surrounded by a bevy of eligible men, Lord Danvers in particular. Even though business called him north, he found he could not leave. The mere chance that Elizabeth would attend one of the social functions crowding his calendar anchored him in town. More often than not, Darcy fought the jealous fire in his soul with alcohol. More brandy and wine bottles were collected in the remaining three weeks of the season than they had in the six months before. By the time he made his way to the Northrups for dinner, he was nearly in his cups.

Caroline crooned seeing her place card next to that of Fitzwilliam Darcy. She was not sure what charm had worked this evening, but she was grateful for the opportunity to slip a few more drops of poison in his ear. She glanced at the elegantly set table. ''Tis nearly done,' she thought. 'He has been unnerved. The more *she* is absent, the more agitated he becomes. I wonder where that simpering Lord Danvers has been keeping himself. No matter, his absence only furthers my intent.'

Commotion at the door announced the arrival of Darcy and his cousin. Caroline maneuvered herself into position. As the men approached the drawing room, Caroline slunk over to him. "Mr. Darcy," she cooed, "how lovely to see you. Your presence will lift this dreary gathering to some semblance of civility. Pray, sir, what has occupied you so?" She batted her eyelashes at the tall, dark gentleman to her right.

"Business, madam," he replied heavily. Dame Agatha was announced, and Darcy's eyes flew to her side, but only her escort, Lord Aubrey stood there. He could not keep disappointment from coursing through him. He sighed and his shoulders fell. Caroline composed herself as best she could, and said in a controlled manner, sotto voce, "I wonder what, or perhaps who, detains the duchess *tonight?*"

Mr. Darcy caught her intended whisper and was about to move away, when Agatha strode up to him. "Darcy, a word?" the Dowager asked.

"Excuse me, Miss Bingley," he said stressing heavily the word *Miss.*

"Of course," she simpered, curtsying to them both. Darcy fought his mind and the image of Danvers entertaining Elizabeth at Wyndom House, alone, while Agatha attended the Northrup's dinner. The couple walked off to a secluded alcove. Darcy surveyed Agatha's countenance. She too, was troubled. "Agatha, what is it?"

"Elizabeth is unable to attend. She *says* it is her head," Agatha began.

"But you do not believe her?" he asked, suspicion and dread crept into his voice. Agatha looked relieved.

"Yes, I mean, no… I fear there is something… she keeps something from me. Not even Jane knows what troubles her."

"Troubles?" This unexpected word cut through Darcy's insecurities.

The older woman only nodded her head. A tear caught her eye, and she quickly wiped it away. "The way she looks at the boys… something is not right, Fitzwilliam, but I am at a loss… she reveals nothing."

The dinner bell rang and the crowd moved towards the hall. Darcy held Agatha back. "I will speak with her Agatha, as soon as I may."

Agatha's eyes revealed her gratitude. As he strode away, she said, "God bless you, Fitzwilliam. Godspeed."

~

Caroline fumed as Darcy made his apologies to the Northrups and departed. She stood by Louisa, unaware of another pair of eyes observing her intently. "I cannot believe it!" Caroline hissed at her sister. "How can he just *leave*! We were to enjoy an evening of conversation!"

"Obviously some important…"

"Harrumph!" Caroline interrupted. "Most likely the Duchess has summoned him, and he runs like a child to his nursemaid…"

"Miss Bingley, Mrs. Hurst, how enchanting to see you here this evening." Lord Malcolm Vreeland approached the couple, an enigmatic smile on his face. He was a tall, thin man with a full head of sandy blond hair. His eyes virtually danced in delight as he approached the women. Behind him, a well-built, impeccably dressed man tagged along. "Please, allow me to introduce my friend, Mr. Robert Smithers. He is a neighbor of mine, in Surrey."

"Mr. Smithers, how lovely to meet you. I, of course, have heard of you, and your exemplary estate, Blathenhause, is it not?"

Flushing with the woman's attention he concurred. "Yes, yes it is. How kind of you mention it."

"Oh, dear sir, how could I not? My friend, Miss Ellis paid a visit recently, and regaled me with tales of its splendor."

"Yes, a veritable Pemberley of the south, no?" Vreeland offered, his eyes innocently awaiting her reaction.

Caroline batted her eyelashes, while Louisa blushed, profusely. She had watched as Vreeland baited her sister, the look in his eye bothering her composure. Lord Vreeland's reputation was well known in the circles she had access to as a married woman. Her maternal instincts told her he meant nothing good for Caroline, so she decided to take action.

"It was a pleasure to make your acquaintance, Lord Vreeland, Mr. Smithers, but if you will excuse us, I must speak with my husband. Caroline?"

Not wishing to leave, Caroline was about to speak, but her sister's pulling on her arm, and the steely look she found in her eyes, kept her silent. "Gentlemen," she offered, in hopes of being coy.

As the ladies made their way across the room, Vreeland watched them with a calculating eye. He then turned abruptly to his companion, "What say you, Robert?"

The shorter man collected his thoughts before replying. When he did, he shook out his arms which had reflexively crossed on his chest. "I agree wholeheartedly, Malcolm. I believe your… proposition is well worth the investment." Vreeland's smile broadened. "I will speak with… the Count… and we shall see… what develops."

~

"Mr. Darcy!" Elizabeth exclaimed in surprise. "What brings you to Wyndon House?"

"I… I anticipated seeing you at the Northrup's this evening. Dame Agatha said a headache kept you home." Elizabeth was dressed in a gown of gold. Her hair was pinned with delicate flowers of topaz. She had taken off her gloves, tossing them across the desk of her study. He noted they lay across crumpled papers scattered about. He caught her in the middle of pacing the room.

"Yes, that is so, sir." He noted the paleness of her complexion and for a moment, his suspicion faltered.

"Nothing else?"

She moved toward the bell pull, but his comment struck her as odd. She clutched her hands together. Darcy noticed a paper she attempted to hide in her hand. "Your meaning escapes me." Something in his manner, his tone, set off her defenses.

"Dame Agatha was concerned." He watched as she abruptly turned her head, one slender hand quickly brought up to rub her neck. "I am sorry I interrupted you..." he indicated the crumpled paper she held. "You were in the midst of reading..." He watched her closely as mortification splayed across her face and it paled before his eyes. Her cheeks were flushed, her eyes petrified, as if she faced walking off the edge of a cliff. 'Something is incredibly wrong here. But what?' In two strides he was before her. He held out his hand for the paper. She snatched her hand away. He stood before her, waiting, his expression brooking no opposition. He took the note, his eyes quickly scanning the page.

While he read, her mind screamed. 'No! This cannot be happening! How can I stop this?' Elizabeth did what she always did when confronting a difficult situation; she bit her lip, and clutched her fingers, pulling them as if to straighten them, and the situation into neat, identifiable lines. 'I cannot...' She hesitated, quickly thinking through the consequences of letting Darcy discover the nature and source of her affairs. 'Could I?' Before she could think through the hazards of seeking his council, he was reading her future.

There in his hand was a note, printed in capital letters. 'SOON MY DEAR, YOU WILL BE MINE. NOTHING WILL THWART MY DESIRE. NO ONE WILL STOP ME, NOT THIS TIME!'

As he read, his heart turned to ash. The jealousy so expertly nurtured by Miss Bingley burst in his heart. He looked to Elizabeth, thousands of scenarios running through his mind. "So, this is how you repay me...? You asked me to wait. I waited. You asked for my patience. I was patient. And while I pine for you… you betray me with another?" He turned running his hand through his hair. "You… you give yourself to another man?" He felt disgusted with her, with himself. He spat, "What they say is true. You do not care. You seek only … bodies… to warm your bed."

Elizabeth's reaction was immediate. Her posture straightened, her eyes snapped to attention. 'What? He thinks…? He thinks this note is from a lover? My lover?' In an attempt to calm her thoughts, she ran a hand over her hair, before responding. "I have no care, Mr. Darcy, for what *others* say about me. Those who know me, know the truth."

"I see…" he looked at her doubting every assumption he ever held about her. "That I never knew you."

She gasped, horrified by all he implied. Her anger flared, consuming her concern. "As you say, sir."

She turned to walk away.

"Elizabeth, please," his heart called out before his pride could reason with him.

Again she turned, this time looking straight at him. "It is so easy for you, is it not? You leave to Pemberley, returning with barely a word and I am left to wonder of your…. regard. Then, based on … one piece of parchment you feel justified in abusing me, in the basest of terms, without offering me a chance to explain. Without one shred of evidence, not one shred of faith in me, you deny the possibility this is something other than the prattle of your mind's delusion." She rubbed a hand across her brow. "I… I have not the time for this, nor the inclination for such theatrics. Good night, sir." With that she left the room, the latch softly clicking as it closed.

Darcy stood, feeling the utter fool until a knock roused him from his thoughts.

"Mr. Darcy? Smothers asked.

"Yes?" Darcy responded, as if coming out of a fog.

"I have called your carriage, sir."

"Very good." Darcy gathered his gloves and hat. Leaving the house, he wondered if he would ever be allowed to return.

~

Jane Bennet was nearly content with the daily running of the Gardiner's household, now that her Aunt Madeline was well into her third pregnancy. She was pleased that Mr. Bingley had been granted permission to court her and had become a constant visitor to Gracechurch Street. Her main concern was that, as her duties there were more strenuous than at Wyndom House, Jane had fewer opportunities to visit Elizabeth, and she worried over her sister's state of mind.

While awaiting a call from Mr. Bingley, Jane's thoughts returned to Elizabeth. 'It is so odd, she sends Georgiana away and then insists that Agatha go and visit Lord Aubrey, and that I come here,' she looked about the sitting room, "and assist Aunt Gardiner."

The opening of the parlour door broke her train of thought and with irritation she focused on the intruder. Mr. Bingley entered, but noticed that her serene countenance was rippled by concern. Quickly he came, taking her hand to his lips, bringing a smile to her lips.

"Jane… Miss Bennet, how are you this fine afternoon?"

"Well, Mr. Bingley, thank you. And you?"

"Well, now that I am at leisure to have the afternoon with you." She blushed at his praise. "Tell me, have you anything in particular you would like to do?"

"As it so happens, sir, I would very much like to take a walk in the park."

~

Jane expertly led them to the wooded walkway that bordered the duck pond. While Mr. Bingley entertained the children, Jane, uncharacteristically let her attention wander to the wilder parts of the glen. It was nearly 3:15 in the afternoon, and Jane was almost certain the shouts of delight emanating from the pond belonged to her nephews. Jane kept her eyes peeled while trying to maintain some semblance of proper decorum.

Seeing the dark coat of a rather tall man standing nearly hidden in the trees, Jane gasped. Her quiet cry alerted Bingley, but before he could speak, Jane had regained her composure, placing a finger to her lips. Her eyes begged him to understand. As Bingley took in the man's stance, his thoughts entertained the notion of Jane's infidelity, but with one glance at his beloved, he realized his error. Jane's eyes were crinkled in confusion, but also in concern. Returning from his initial train of thought, Bingley looked around, realizing that Jane had brought them there with the intent of witnessing what lay before them. His eyes scanned through the trees, to the duck pond and the scampering children at the water's edge. When recognition dawned upon him, he too, gasped. Jane turned, and hissed, "Shhhh."

"Elizabeth?" he asked, comprehending Jane's concern. Jane pleased with his conclusion, nodded, and pulled him by the arm to join her young cousins.

"Trust me?" he asked her.

"Implicitly," she whispered.

"I believe letting him know that we have seen him, may scare him off, eh?"

Jane did not voice her doubt, but hesitation was written on her face.

"Trust me, Jane. We will not confront him. Perhaps some good will come from letting him know he has been observed." Taking a moment to look him in the eye, making sure he realized the gravity of the situation, she nodded.

"Grayson, Clara, come quickly." He called to the Gardiner children, who scampered eagerly towards them.

Bingley spoke up. "Children, your cousins Ian and Rafael are there, by the duck pond. Why do you not run and join them?" They turned to find the path, he quickly called them back. "No, I think this time you may cut through the wood, here, this way."

Looking for Jane's permission, they ran off towards the water. Waiting a full count of ten, Bingley called out, "Children, wait for us! Come my dear, let us make haste before our charges outrun us." Taking her by the hand, he pulled her through the woods until they came within five feet of the tall, dark man who still stood vigil against a tree. While Jane kept her eyes on the children, Bingley made direct eye contact, nodding as they progressed toward the open meadow. The man startled as they passed close by. He stood at attention, but before his suspicion could form, the couple had rejoined the Gardiner children now speaking with their cousins. Fortunately, their sentinel was at a distance and could not hear the cheery reunion. The Gardiners and Gainsbridges played happily until a spring downpour forced everyone to run for their carriages.

∾

The next day, Charles Bingley sat sipping port in Darcy's study. He had had a most frustrating morning when he and Jane had called upon her sister. Hoping to offer their support and information regarding the tall dark stranger stalking the Gainsbridge children, they were stymied when she flatly refused to discuss the matter with them and had dismissed them, claiming a headache required her immediate sequestration in her chambers.

"Damn imperious, too..." Bingley snorted before taking a full measure of his port.

Looking at him curiously, Darcy said, "I do believe, Charles that this has been the longest you have managed to remain silent, ever!"

Unable to return the humor sparking in his friend's eyes, Charles only turned his head to the fire.

"Come off it, Charles. You might as well tell me. Save a bit of time in the long run."

"No, I am sorry, Darce, but I have been sworn to secrecy."

Darcy lifted one brow.

"No, do not tempt me. Jane... Miss Bennet would have my head..."

Instantly Darcy's body straightened. "Charles," he growled. "What is it?"

Looking at his friend, Charles's eyes widened. "No, I am afraid..." his conscience got the better of him and leaning forward he demanded. "But you must *promise* me that you will not go off on a tear, Darcy." He waited. "Promise?"

"I... I... cannot."

"You must. I need your advice, *and* your discretion."

"What is it, Charles?"

"Darcy..."

'Oh, alright, Bingley. I promise. I promise not to go off without a full understanding. Are you satisfied?"

Relieved, Bingley continued. "The other day..." and for the next hour Charles related his experience in the park. While Bingley relayed the initial conversation propelling Jane to the park the day before, Darcy sat, his hand held to his mouth. 'Who could this be?' he pondered. 'And what can it mean?' Briefly the image of a crumpled piece of parchment ran through his mind, but was overwhelmed by the burning desire to know who was this mysterious stranger was, and what was his connection to the House of Gainsbridge.

Interrupting Bingley's narrative, Darcy asked, "And Jane, Miss Bennet, she does not know who this man could be?"

"No," Charles replied, emphatically. "The poor girl tried to place his features, but to no avail."

"He resembles none of the callers to her sister?"

Bingley looked at his friend askance. "Visitors? How would Miss Bennet know who calls upon her sister?" Darcy looked astonished at this question. Bingley replied, slowly. "Darcy, Jane resides in Cheapside, at the home of her Aunt and Uncle Gardiner. She has for weeks now."

"Yes," Darcy thought for a moment, wondering why he thought she was at Wyndom House. "You mentioned that, did you not?"

"Yes, yes I did, although I do wish she were at Wyndom." Darcy's brow arched at his friend's statement. "Do not look at *me* that way, Darcy. It is not disdain for a man of trade. No, I would prefer Jane, Miss Bennet stay with her sister, because her sister, something bothers Lady Elizabeth and it bothers Miss Bennet that she knows not the root of her concern."

"Perhaps it is a personal matter?"

Looking at his friend as if he had gown a second head, Bingley replied, as one would a child, "Darcy, those two share everything."

The dark brow rose again. "Perhaps Lady Elizabeth feels Miss Bennet would think less of her if she knew the truth."

Bingley gaped at his friend. "Fitzwilliam Darcy! I cannot believe you of all people would say such a thing."

"No? It is no worse than what I hear from your sister."

Again Bingley sat, stupefied at the turn in the conversation. "And from *her* I expect such falsehoods. And I ignore her when she spouts such nonsense." A strange look came over Bingley. "Darcy, you do not *believe* Caroline, do you?"

Darcy looked down, unable to face his friend. "You do! My good Lord, you do!" It was Bingley's turn to look away. After taking longer than a moment to compose himself, he turned back to his friend and said, "Darcy, I have yet to meet a woman with the strength, intelligence and *integrity* of Elizabeth Gainsbridge. If you were anyone else, I would call you out."

"Many a man has been betrayed by a pretty face, Charles. You of all men should know that."

Rising, Bingley placed his glass on the side table, and straightened his spine. "I see. No," he held out his hand, palm up. "Do not bother. I know the way." He turned and walked to the door. "All I will say on this

William, is that you are wrong. Your vision is clouded. Lady Elizabeth is honorable, and you are a fool to let the petty manipulations of my sister convince you otherwise." He reached for the door, then turned. "I wonder William, why it is, of all the women my sister has maligned, that it is this one, a woman who would match you at every point, that you are willing to believe of her the worst? Answer me this, why you are so adamant to believe Caroline's lies?"

The door latch clicked shut, leaving Darcy the long, darkening afternoon to ask himself the self same question.

~

Several weeks later, Elizabeth paced her study late into the night, her desk nearly covered with crumpled pieces of paper. A half written letter lay on its surface, her quill carelessly thrown across the parchment. Her thoughts had long ago turned into fear. Now they overwhelmed her. Exhausted after weeks of sleepless nights, she threw herself upon the sofa and sobbed. She indulged in tears, until the sleep that had eluded her finally rescued her.

In the morning, she dressed quickly, gathered her boys, and left Wyndom House.

~

~ CHAPTER NINE ~

June, 1812
Darcy House, London

Charles Bingley was prepared to enjoy his first evening in company in nearly a fortnight. After speaking with Jane and allowing her gentle spirit to calm his agitation, he had forgiven Darcy his slight of Lady Elizabeth's character. Nevertheless, he was mildly unsettled at this, their first evening in each other's company since he had uncharacteristically walked out on his friend. It was one of the Darcy's last evenings in town before returning to Pemberley and Bingley was insistent that he and his friend end the season on good terms. As the Bingleys, Hursts and Darcys settled into the parlor for conversation, Darcy's butler appeared at the door attempting to catch his employer's attention.

"Excuse me, Bingley, Hurst, I will be but a minute." He rose to follow his man out into the hall surprised when his major duomo shut the door behind them. Waiting there in his hallways was a very agitated Duchess of Leicester.

"Agatha!?" Darcy began, his tone stiff and formal. "To what do I owe the pleasure of your…"

"Have you seen Elizabeth? Is she here?" Agatha's distress was extreme and her words tumbled one onto the other. "Have you heard from her? Do you know where she may be?"

Looking at his unexpected guest, Darcy was confused and angry that she could presume that Elizabeth would be with him. "I believe Darcy House would be the last place…" pain seared his heart. "There are others …"

"Ah, yes, the wolves howling at the gate… as if *they* would be of any use…" Agatha spat.

He turned to face her, his eyes blazing in anger. There was nothing more he could say. Refocusing, she came up to him, grasping his arms as if it were a life line thrown to her as she drowned at sea, she repeated, "Darcy! I beg of you… have you seen her? Has she been here at all? Do you know where she has gone?"

Of all the things she could have said, these words chilled him to his core. He felt anger at her desertion of first him and now Agatha crackle through his veins, his love morphing into a dagger stabbing at his heart. "I believe I am the *last* man she would trust with that information. As I said, there are others…" The pain in Darcy's heart broke through the disdain in his voice as he barely eked out. "To whom she now turns."

Agatha released him as if touching him burned her fingers, or perhaps soiled them.

"I refer you to Lord Danvers. It is widely known that *he* is still welcome at Wyndon." Darcy made absolutely no attempt to mask the pain and bitterness in his voice.

"Lord Danvers!?" Agatha finally added. "I fail to take your meaning..."

Regaining her focus, Agatha made to take her leave. "I have no time for this. I had hoped..."

"Agatha, I never thought you to be one for melodramatics..."

"Darcy," Agatha turned on him, her voice now full of steel. "Elizabeth is missing! She and the boys! They are gone! They left no word."

Darcy stood absolutely still, trying to digest the information.

"No one has seen or heard from her in two days." Agatha cried to the silent man.

Taken aback, he shook his head, admitting he had lost her. "I do not know, Agatha."

Agatha recoiled from him as if his skin was vile. "Darcy," she gasped.

"She has admirers..." he retreated to his pain, his shoulders slumped. "Question the others."

Agatha stared at him until he looked up, cutting into his façade of the jilted lover. "Enough!" she growled." He looked up at her and they stood glaring at each other until fear regained its hold on Agatha. With panic guiding her words she mumbled, "I thought she would... perhaps Longbourn? Her father is not well... but then..." she turned and walked back towards her host. "Darcy, you… of all people know that for a woman, the world is not as safe as it appears. Especially for a woman of fortune… great fortune."

Recalling Rafael's impassioned plea to protect Elizabeth, Darcy's guilt began to struggle against his jealousy. "Agatha, please! Calm yourself. Tell me what has happened."

"I need your help, Darcy."

Again Darcy tried to master his emotions. "Agatha?" he noted that her agitation only grew, pushing his jealousy into a small corner of his heart. Recognizing the need for a more private interview, Darcy headed for his study. He opened the door and waited for the Duchess to enter. "Now, Agatha, tell me all."

Taking a strengthening breath Agatha began pacing as she spoke. "I know not how to begin. I… was in Kent, visiting Aubrey at his estate… Queensdown. Elizabeth did not accompany me as Jane remains in town. I should have known…" She looked directly at Darcy. Seeing his need for clarification, she added. "She's been agitated for weeks now. I should have guessed… Elizabeth's questions about him, what I knew, what Georgiana knew. We tried to refocus her, but she would not let it drop. I was hoping she had escaped… here…" looking at his confused face, she pulled a small bundle of folded parchment from her reticule and handed it to Darcy.

"I beg you, Agatha, spare me letters from her lovers…"

Faster than he could have imagined, the elderly woman crossed the few feet between them, her hand soundly slapping the younger man's face. Her eyes blazed indignation and fury. She thrust the first crumpled letter into his hand. It was in Elizabeth's hand. "Lovers indeed!" Agatha growled. "If only you behaved like a true lover!" His heart shattered as he read the little she had written,

"Mr. Darcy,

Please do not disregard this missive. I need your help. I beg you, please... "

The water stains dappled across the page seeped into his soul. 'Her tears!' Elizabeth wrote of the half dozen attempts at contacting him. Agitatedly, he shuffled through the papers, all addressed to him. All were crumpled to be discarded. None were complete.

"She is gone, Darcy." Both stood in silence, until Agatha's composure broke. Her words tumbled out. "Elizabeth gave Mrs. Bates a fortnight's vacation. She said Bates had earned some time away from the boys. When I returned, Meersham told me that she released her maid as well, and... well, he thought she was coming to Kent, to surprise me. But when I returned this afternoon, he... he was very concerned. Together we tried to make sense of it all, but have come up with naught." Agatha's agitation increased. "He told me of the rumors..."

"What rumors?" Darcy asked with great intensity.

"Among the staff. Mrs. Bates... has for some time believed that someone has been following her and the boys." She pulled another stack of notes from her reticule. "Meersham says that since I have been away, these have come. One hand delivered, every other day. All unsigned. All threatening."

Darcy read the notes. The earlier ones were printed in block letters, but the most recent letters reverted to script, a familiar script that had plagued the Darcy House for years. Fury blazed in Darcy's soul as he hissed, "Wickham."

Agatha's voice cracked and she swayed, "The boys!" Darcy felt the room spin as he tried to claim his sanity, her letter still in his hands.

There was a gentle knock on the door, before it quickly opened, "I heard Dame… Agatha!" The girl ran to the older woman, kneeling at her feet. "What is it?" Georgiana looked at her brother, who was ashen. Slowly, he walked to the door, closing it as Bingley's head popped in.

"Darcy, is everything…?" He looked in at the Duchess. "Dame Agatha? Are you well?"

Darcy allowed Charles entrance, then turned and locked the door, just as Caroline Bingley rounded the corner. Without speaking another word, Darcy went to his desk, taking pen to paper, composing a note to Colonel Fitzwilliam. As he did, Bingley was consoling the women as best he could. Rather than speak, she showed him the notes, then gave the letters to Georgiana. Looking up Darcy cringed as Georgiana gasped recognizing the danger of the situation. All three turned as Darcy rang for a servant.

"What will be done, Fitzwilliam?" Georgiana cried trying to calm the panic she felt overwhelming her.

"All that may be done, poppet," Darcy rose from his desk, coming to her. If she had been able to see beyond her fear, she would have noticed the defeated manner in which he moved.

"Darcy, Dame Agatha, do the Bennets... does Jane... Miss Bennet know?" Bingley asked.

A look of horror spread across three faces, each recoiling at the task of informing Jane that her precious sister had been kidnapped, along with her sons. "I will go to Gracechurch Street, immediately." Bingley said, energized by having something to contribute to the calamity.

"Charles, please, tell Jane of this. If she is able would you bring her back to Wyndom? Elizabeth will need her." Agatha said. Bingley nodded before leaving to collect his sisters. When he did, silence filled the room until Georgiana rose to her feet.

"I will have Emily prepare a bag," she said still shaken. Heading toward the door, she stopped and turned to her brother. "I shall stay with Dame Agatha until Elizabeth is found. Agatha nodded, her eyes softening, her lips forming the closest resemblance to a smile, her first since returning to London.

The silence returned, heavy on the remaining occupants of the room. Darcy walked to the window, gazing out, trying to order his thoughts.

'Elizabeth! Wickham has Elizabeth!' was all his mind could say. "I am sorry, Agatha. I should have..."

"Rafael charged you with their welfare, William! Her welfare! You should have seen to her long ago." Agatha rose and walked toward him waving the notes in front of her. "Rafael trusted you! He had faith that you would see beyond your own, selfish desires to honor and protect her. She was more than a wife, William, she was his salvation." Agatha's voice crackled with emotion. "Elizabeth brought light and life into our lives. She gave us the hope of her children and when Rafael knew he could not longer care for her, he came to you. His best friend on this earth and gave her care to you. I know she was not receptive to this at first, but she did come to rely on you. For the boys, and for herself." Darcy hung his head. Remorse overpowered them both. "We failed her, Fitzwilliam. You and I…"

"I… we quarreled, I was not ready to… I thought she would refuse me."

"Refuse you! Darcy! She needed your help! My help! She is not yet one and twenty! Surely you recall what it is to be the master of an estate and responsible for the youngest members of your family! And *you* were born to it. Elizabeth has had but a mere three years to acclimate to being wife, mother and widow, as well as Mistress of Crystalglen." Agatha agitatedly paced the room until her agony broke through. Her sobs, starting as a moan, filled the room. She staggered to the nearest chair. "My God! What am I to do? She is all that is left to me." For a moment she was lost in her grief, and could speak no more. Darcy could only look on; guilt battering what was left of his heart. His entire world lay shattered at his feet.

"We failed her, Darcy. Shame on me, and shame on you."

'How could I have gone to her? That note!' The veil of jealousy finally lifted and Darcy stiffened. 'It spoke not of love… it was a threat. She told me there was another meaning! But I would not listen. If my temper was not so overbearing… then perhaps…'

"I will leave you, now, William." She moved towards the door to leave. "Go back to the Caroline Bingleys of this world. Leave Elizabeth to me. I will deal with this as well as I can."

"Agatha, no! I beg you, stay!" Darcy stopped her by the door which she was about to open. The older woman looked into his soul. She saw his grief and regret yet was unwilling to relent. "I am ashamed." He looked up and took a full breath. "Please, I beg of you, allow me… to help. I will find Elizabeth. Please."

Agatha allowed Darcy to lead her back to her chair. "When Mrs. Bates told Elizabeth her concerns, Elizabeth became frightened, doubling the guards that always accompanied the boys." Agatha looked to William, her mouth gaping. "She knew! She knew already!" escaped her trembling lips. "She knew and was already protecting the boys."

"For over a month?" Darcy asked, interrupting Agatha.

"Then what? What could have caused her to panic so and leave the house?"

Darcy cast his mind back to the increasing strain and fatigue that plagued Elizabeth that he had ascribed to a more licentious cause. As if snapping out of a dream, Darcy asked. "You said she was guarded?"

"She was. They were."

"Then we should start questioning them."

"They are gone!"

Darcy was incredulous and he just stared at her. "Gone? But how?"

"I know not how, the driver, the guards, even the carriage are all gone, missing still." She broke into tears again, and Darcy went to the sideboard to pour a snifter of brandy. When he handed it to her, she said, "Thank you."

A knock on the door, interrupted further conversation. At first Darcy was disinclined to answer, but Hastings was at the door announcing, "Lord Aubrey, to see the Duchess of Leicester, sir."

Darcy quickly walked to the door. There stood his butler, Lord Aubrey directly behind him. "Darcy."

"Sir."

"Agatha is here?"

"Edwin! Thank you for coming!" Agatha replied rising from her chair.

"Agatha, I came as soon as I got your message." Aubrey went to her. "Smothers said you were here. What has happened?!"

"Elizabeth and the boys, they have been taken!"

"What? How can that be?"

"George Wickham has them," she said trying desperately to maintain her composure.

"You are sure?"

She nodded. "He sent these." She handed him the notes. After reading them quickly, he sniffed the paper. "How many people have touched these?"

"Elizabeth, I believe, and Smothers, myself..."

"I have handled them, as has Bingley, and Georgiana." Darcy added.

Aubrey sighed in discontent before reading them again. "These stains, the randomness suggests..."

"Tears," Agatha responded, her own eyes grieving for Elizabeth.

Looking at his cousin, he recalled the vivacious woman who had brightened all their lives. Aubrey attempted to control his emotions. Focusing on the paper still in his hands, the latest threat, he rumbled aloud. "Is this Elizabeth's hand?" he asked his cousin who nodded. "He demands of her 30,000 pounds..."

"Georgiana's dowry!" Darcy gasped. Agitation overcame him; he paced the room like a caged tiger. "You must let me..."

"It is not the money, man. I... what if he has done her harm? Or the boys? Those poor lambs! They are all that is left of Rafael!" Here Agatha lost her composure collapsing on the chair.

"Agatha!" Darcy knelt before her. "I promise you, on all that I hold dear that I *will* find Elizabeth. And if he," Darcy could not control the tremor that seized his hands. "If he has harmed her, or the boys, I swear I shall..."

Agatha took hold of his hands. When she saw the fire and resolve in his eyes, she relaxed. He willed her to understand his devotion to Elizabeth and her children.

"I will not fail her this time, Agatha. I swear to you."

Agatha gave a faint smile and nodded.

"How was this delivered?" Aubrey interrupted holding up the ransom notes.

"I believe by messenger." Agatha tore her eyes from Darcy's reassuring gaze. "Yes, Rundle gave him a coin for his trouble, and the lad seemed quite pleased."

"Rundle spoke with him?" Aubrey looked hopeful.

"Yes, he did."

"Excellent. Than we shall adjourn to Wyndom House and speak with the good man."

"What may I do to help, Agatha? Lord Aubrey?" Darcy was frantic to be included in Elizabeth's recovery.

"Pray, man. Get on your knees and pray."

Darcy looked so stricken, that even Agatha's heavy heart held pity for him. Turning to her cousin she said, "He knows Wickham, Edwin. They grew up together."

Aubrey's eyebrows rose. "This is true?"

"Yes, sir. We did."

"Excellent. Than you may come with us. Quickly."

"Georgiana! Call for her, tell her to hurry." Agatha spoke to Darcy. The trio was out in the hall, heading for the front foyer.

"No need, I am ready," Georgiana rose from the chair in which she waited for her elders.

"She has offered to stay with me until Elizabeth is found," Agatha whispered to her cousin. The older man looked approvingly at the young woman. He took her hand, bowed over it and gently laid a kiss upon it.

"As the nearest blood relation to my dear Agatha, I thank you, dear lady. You will ease my mind, greatly."

Georgiana smiled and curtsied to the older man, then took the arm he offered. With Agatha on his other they set off for their carriages. Darcy was left, alone, bringing up the rear.

He called back to his man, "If word comes from Bingley, forward it to the Wyndom House. The same for Fitzwilliam."

With that, they were off.

~ CHAPTER TEN ~

June, 1812
Belmont Estate, Essex

It was nearly dusk when Elizabeth awoke. She surveyed the desolate room, haven for her and her sons for the last three days. Scrambling to her feet, she felt relief as two pair of small hands held on to her ferociously. She dropped to her knees, arms full of her boys. In the fading light she saw their tear-stained faces and she held them, thanking God that they were still alive and unharmed. Gaining strength, Elizabeth pulled away to again search for a way out.

"Mamma!" Ian cried. "Hungry."

"Me too," replied his brother in a whisper.

"Oh, my darlings, let us find what we may." She could not let go their hands. They clung to each other as they walked over to the table where sat a loaf of stale bread and brown-tinged apples. "At least he feeds us," she said, pulling the chair out. Sitting herself down, she pulled her children to her lap. She took another moment hugging them close to her chest, tears of relief still streaming down her cheek, 'we are together!' As she broke the bread into pieces, Elizabeth continued scanning the room. Though normally picky eaters, the boys gobbled the bread and the browned apple with relish. Elizabeth nibbled her piece. While hungry herself, she wanted her children to have more, unsure when their next meal would come. She repositioned them on the chair and walked to the window.

Her bruises were healing and Elizabeth could walk without pain. With a hand resting on her waist she felt a burn where Wickham had pushed her against the wall retaliating for the bite she had taken out of his lip. Her cheek still stung from the punch and she was unsure if there was discoloration. Looking out the window, she noticed a wooded glen not too far off. 'I may make it out, after dark, but how do I get down from the second story, with two boys? And Wickham? Would he trust someone to work with him?' Elizabeth tried to focus, recalling everything she had heard about her captor from either her husband or Georgiana. She recalled Rafael telling her that Wickham was 'clever, but not smart. A loner and lazy, preferring the easy way of things,' she added wondering how this information could help her present situation. 'And he has a gun.' The hope her recollections had stirred drained when she also remember that that was all she was sure of. That and her two year old sons while very brave, were not much help.

'What can I use?' she thought quickly. She looked up and out the window, to the roof. 'It is not very far! Perhaps I could climb…' but then one of the boys, Ian, began to whimper, and she realized that climbing over twenty feet, with two squirming boys was truly not an option. She sat on the sill, sighing, until her eye was caught by a rusted piece of metal dangling off the side of the house, only three feet away. Holding on to the side of the windowsill, she reached for it, and was amazed that when she swung back into the room, a two-foot piece of metal was clasped in her hand. She smiled, and her boys smiled back.

Elizabeth tested the weight of the metal by banging it in her hand. "Ouch!" she said, pulling her hand back and shaking it. She moved towards her boys who held out their arms for her. They kissed her palm, as she had done so many times for them, until they heard footsteps approaching. The boys grew frightened, and Elizabeth tried to quiet them.

"Hush, my darlings. You must be very, very good," she whispered urgently. You *must* listen, and do exactly as I say. Agreed?" she asked.

"Yes, mamma," they replied nearly in unison.

"Stay here, then, and pay close attention to what I say. But do not look at me!" she whispered as she moved to the wall to the left of the door. The door swung open, and there stood George Wickham, his cravat undone, his eyes bleary. He looked at the boys, and over to where Elizabeth had earlier slept. He stepped forward, then swaggered as the metal crashed down upon his head. Again the metal crashed on to his head and he fell to the ground. The gun he held in his hand fired as it hit the floor and Elizabeth felt rage rise in her breast. The metal fell from her hand now clenched in a fist. Falling to her knees, Elizabeth felt her rage consume her and she struck the man on the floor.

When she could strike no more, she looked up at her children who stood frightened alongside the wooden table. Quickly, Elizabeth bent her head to Wickham's chest to ascertain that the man still breathed. Ripping her petticoat she quickly tied his hands behind his back. She then picked up the gun and threw it out the window as far away as possible. She grabbed her stunned children, hugging them tightly before taking their hands and heading down the stairs. Their little legs flew, but not fast enough for Elizabeth. Scooping Ian up into her arms, he was always the more timid of the two, she smiled as best she could to encourage Rafael to hurry. The clatter of his small shoes on the wooden stairs kept pace with her own, hurried step. Her gaze alternated with locating the nearest door, paying close attention Rafe did not fall and looking over her shoulder should Wickham escape his bonds.

Two horses were the sole occupants of the decrepit stable. Never being a great horsewoman, Elizabeth still felt it was the quickest way to reach civilization, so she improvised a saddle, and perched her two sons atop the beast. She then hoisted herself up riding astride, her skirts hiked indecently to her thigh. She rode as fast as she could on the third rate horse through the woods. She rode, looking for water, recalling Rafael tell her of the times he had gotten lost on his rambles, knowing that once he found running water, people could not be far behind. Elizabeth only hoped that the people she found would be willing and able to help.

As they rode she could feel her little ones beginning to nod off. She called to them, trying to keep them awake. "My darlings, you must stay awake, at least until we reach safety. Please, angels. Stay with mamma." She called out to them, urging them to sing the songs Mrs. Bates had taught them. They recited rhymes, and Elizabeth began listing the names of the Roman emperors and the British kings. They rode for nearly an hour, through the darkening night, the chill of the wind helping the boys in their struggle to remain awake. Finally, exhaustion over took them, and as Ian slouched left, Rafael leaned too far to the right and his mother, grabbing the sleeve of one child nearly missed catching the other. Unfortunately, the horse did not miss an uneven patch in the path and stumbled. Their screams bounced through the forest, a beacon to friend and foe alike.

As soon as she could, Elizabeth gathered her sons to her, whispering, "Ian, Rafael, are you well?" They whimpered in their fright. "Can you stand, my loves?" They nodded their curly heads, and each taking hold of their mother's hands proceeded on foot.

"Horsey, mama?" Ian asked gently, pulling his mother's attention back to the animal lying on its side, its foot at an unnatural angle. Elizabeth grew frantic. The horse would be of no additional use to her or her children. She was alone, in the woods, unsure of where they were and night was approaching. Panic began to rise in her breast, her breath cut short as fear took hold of her. Grabbing her children's hands, she rose preparing to flee.

"Allow me to assist you, Duchess," Wickham sneered atop his nag. Elizabeth stilled, as her fear turned to fury. With a quietude she had never felt before, she rose, in one fluid moment pushed her children behind her skirts, protecting them with her body. That Wickham appreciated the gesture was evident in the smirk stretching his lips. He had his pistol pulled from his holster pointing it at each child as he poked his head out from her skirts. Elizabeth's eyes narrowed, her hands clenched at her side. First Rafael, then Ian braved their face out from the silk gown of their mother, only to quickly duck back behind her knees. Elizabeth stepped back, her hands pressing her children again behind her. Wickham chuckled, then cocked his pistol, and having aimed at each child, turned his attention and fired one shot into the horse's chest. The boys screamed and Elizabeth, seizing her chance, ran. Adrenaline fueled their escape as the boys struggled to keep up with their mother as she led them deeper into the forest.

Kicking his heels into his mount, Wickham set off for them, his eyes scanning for his prey among the growing shadows. Feeling her heart in her chest Elizabeth ran until she felt her left arm pull earthward and then release. "Ian!" she screamed without thought, whipping herself and Rafael around to find her fallen child.

"Mama!" the child called out. Elizabeth was on her knees, her arms wrapped around Ian, Rafael hugging his short arms around them both. When she released him, Ian crumpled to the ground.

"Hurts, Mama," he said stroking his ankle.

They heard a rushing whirl approach, but before they could move the tall shadow of a man was off his horse and embracing them. Pushing back, instinctively pummeling him with their collective fists, none of the Gainsbridges stopped until Darcy pulled back and they could see his face in the dimming light. As recognition dawned on her, Elizabeth felt herself pulled back into his safe embrace. She held on to him, unable to let him go. Relief coursed through her and she slumped as his arms wrapped around her and her children. They whimpered into his waistcoat and Elizabeth felt her tears soak into the fine wool of his jacket.

Suddenly Darcy's ears pricked, and his head shot up. He stood, dragging Elizabeth and the boys into a standing position. Copying Elizabeth's earlier movements, he pushed them all behind his back. Elizabeth placed her children behind them both as she stood by his side.

"Is this not a fine picture of domestic solidarity?" Wickham held a pistol in each hand as his horse gently walked toward them. "It is so like *you*, Darcy, to come in and pick up another man's mess."

"What do you want, Wickham?" Darcy barked, stepping forward to further protect the Gainsbridges from their assailant. He knew even Wickham's aim was true at this close distance. His only hope was distraction.

"I want what is my due."

Keeping pace with him as Wickham circled, Darcy asked, "And what could that possibly be?"

"Why, what every man wants… a home of his own, money in his purse, a wife, sons…"

Elizabeth felt her blood turn cold.

"I have compromised the Duchess." Wickham said nonchalantly, as if holding all the cards.

Darcy gasped. Elizabeth cried out, "No! That is a lie!"

"She will marry me," he laughed maliciously. "I would have been content with that simpering sister of yours, Darcy. But her Grace here saw fit to interfere. Therefore, it is only right *she* compensate me; a bride for a bride. Think of it as interest that will compound *daily*." His tone left no doubt to his intent.

Darcy clenched his jaw and fist. Thinking of ways to distract Wickham, he said, "You will have to kill me first, Wickham."

"As you wish." Wickham took aim at the tall man once as close as a brother. The sound of metal clicking into place echoed about the trees as each pistol readied itself to fire. Seizing the only advantage available, Darcy charged the hindquarters of the horse, slapping its backside as hard as he could. The horse bucked and began to run. Darcy pushed Elizabeth and the boys to the ground after they had rushed behind the nearest tree. He pulled out a pistol from his boot. Wickham pulled at the reins, bringing the horse about with a cruel yank. Quickly regaining control of his mount, and his sense, Wickham growled, searching for Darcy in the growing darkness. Finding his target he pointed his gun at Darcy's chest. A shot rang out. Wickham's gun discharged into the trees as he fell from his horse.

Red coats flushed the area. Wickham was handcuffed before being led away, bleeding.

Darcy was on his knees, Elizabeth and her boys gathered in his strong arms. He covered her hair with kisses. Tears fell freely until she pushed back and looked him in the eye. She searched his face before clasping him to her. She kissed him long and hard, pulling him into her, pouring all her emotions, as wild and tumultuous as they were, into him.

Colonel Fitzwilliam approached, and seeing them, stood guard until they required air.

"Your Grace, are you harmed?" he asked.

She looked up from the arms that still clung to her, to her young sons who were feeling strong enough to peep out from her side, to the soldiers securing the area. Darcy rose and aided Elizabeth's assent. She looked at him and found the love and care she had doubted and fought. She clasped his hands and keeping her eyes on Darcy, replied, "I am well, Colonel Fitzwilliam, I am well." Finally she turned to him. "But I would like to go home."

A horse was found for Elizabeth. When safely in the saddle, both boys were hoisted up to her. Although not the most comfortable of seats, she was loathe to relinquish them from her embrace and they were just as determined to remain with her. Darcy's horse returned at his master's call. Darcy rode next to Elizabeth, keeping a watchful eye on her and her precious cargo.

They rode to the nearest town where rooms were quickly found, and messengers dispatched to Agatha, Longbourn and Gracechurch Street heralding the good news of their recovery. After agreeing to meet Colonel Fitzwilliam at the local militia's camp, Darcy cradled Ian and accompanied Elizabeth and Rafael to her rooms, where they nestled the boys into their beds. Before he could depart, Elizabeth placed her hand on his arm.

"Mr. Darcy... Fitzwilliam... I know not how to thank you, but I... if it is not asking too much, I would beg a word with you tomorrow morning?"

"Of course... Elizabeth."

She smiled at him, her hand rising to gently remove a curl falling across his eyes. Her hand slid to gently stroke his cheek, and Darcy wanted nothing more than to take her in his arms again and keep her there forever.

"Until tomorrow, then?"

"Until the morning. Sleep well, El..." he checked for her reaction before repeating, "Elizabeth. If you need anything, do not hesitate to call."

She nodded and looked about the room, lit by only two candles allowing the boys their rest. Darcy knew he should quit the room, but could not. "Elizabeth?"

She looked at him, quickly.

"I am so sorry..."

"Sorry? You saved us!"

"I should have come sooner. This... this is all my fault."

"No, it is not, Fitzwilliam." She had her hands on his arms, holding his attention as he tried to slip into guilt. "Wickham was bent on revenge. You heard him. He had me marked. If not this, he would have attempted something else. At least he took us together. I shudder to think what would have happened if he took only the boys." She broke down as horror overcame her. Instinctively Darcy pulled her close to him, holding her tightly as sobs wracked her body. "Oh, Fitzwilliam! I was so frightened!" She managed between sobs. Darcy cradled her head with one hand, as he gently rocked them in unison.

"Stay with me, please. Do not go!"

"I must, Elizabeth. I need to speak with the Colonel."

"Colonel Fitzwilliam? Can not he wait till morning?"

"No, the colonel of the regiment that holds Wickham. Let me go, quickly, and I shall return as soon as may be. And Elizabeth?" here he pulled her back enough to look into her still teary eyes. "Then I will not leave you, ever. Nothing, nor anyone else will ever come between us, *ever* again."

She sniffled. "Promise?" Darcy believed he could hear the child within her speak.

"I do. I promise. We are together now, for always."

"Then go. I will wait for you."

He kissed her gently, tenderly, and then made for the door. Before exiting completely, he looked at her small frame, again, drinking in the details of the woman he loved.

~

Darcy walked into the commanding officer's study, unsure what he would find. He had disregarded the colonel's orders to desist for the evening, to regroup the following morning. 'And I am ever so grateful that I did,' he thought regarding the gathered men.

Colonel McGuire, Lord Aubrey and Colonel Fitzwilliam looked up from their brandy at the latest arrival.

"There you are Darcy," Colonel McGuire called out, while indicating to his adjunct to pour another glass. The lieutenant brought over a snifter. The colonel continued. "My compliments to you for totally disobeying my command." He walked toward the civilian, "however, if you were in uniform, I would have you in irons."

"Then I thank heavens, I am not, but I am grateful to you and your men." He took the glass, downing it in one shot. "Where is he now?"

"Where the cur belongs, in the goal, after being treated to a deserter's welcome."

At his look of incomprehension, his cousin interjected, "Let me only say that no man in uniform looks kindly on a deserter. And the occasion of his reunion will… discharge… some of that displeasure."

"I was unaware he was in service," Darcy said, thoughtfully.

Colonel McGuire took up the narrative. "Seems Wickham purchased a Lieutenant's commission only a fortnight ago."

Darcy looked up in confusion. Turning to his cousin he asked, "But why?"

"Perhaps as insurance? Who knows what motivates scum."

Colonel McGuire gave his lieutenant leave to speak. "Beggin' your pardon, Colonel, sir, but it seems Lieutenant Wickham used the uniform to impress the ladies... and found the locals most obliging, if you take my meaning, sir."

Both Darcy and Fitzwilliam exchanged knowing glances. Darcy spoke again. "What happens next?"

"A courts martial shall be convened. As we are near enough to war, the penalty shall be very harsh, indeed."

"Could not come for a more deserving man." Colonel Fitzwilliam took another hefty gulp of the liquor.

"Quite. I am afraid however, there will be little enough left of him to bring to trial in a regular court."

At Darcy's raised brow, Colonel McGuire continued. "We have jurisdiction only over his desertion," here he pointed his glass at Darcy before continuing. "During a time of war... conduct unbecoming an officer. Her Grace must see to the charges of kidnapping."

"I will see to that," Aubrey piped in. "Regardless of your... future alliance with Elizabeth, as Agatha's relation, it falls to me."

Darcy nodded his consent.

"Well that settles it, then. Except to hear your tale, Darcy!" Colonel McGuire now had an appealing smile on his face now.

Taking a deep gulp of the fine brandy, 'no doubt a spoil of war,' he thought, Darcy began. "I left you, Fitzwilliam, Aubrey, here with Colonel McGuire, saying I would retire. But I could not. I knew Wickham was using the Belmont farm as he had during our Cambridge days. I had to... I could not rest knowing..." he pulled himself away from the despair he had felt knowing Elizabeth was in Wickham's power.

"I rode through the forest. I would ride there often before dawn, seeking to escape the all night gaming Wickham would host. I heard a shot and then a scream, a woman's... Elizabeth's... and then the cries of her boys. I rode towards the sound and found them. Ian had fallen, twisted his ankle. I had them in my arms when he came upon us. He would have killed me, forced Elizabeth to wed." Darcy's countenance became wild as his hand raked through his hair. "If not... if not..." Darcy looked to McGuire.

"For your cousin's quick thinking, man." McGuire picked up the story. "He was the one to check on you, not trusting you to follow orders.

Colonel Fitzwilliam looked into his glass, contemplating the amber swirls. His eyes shot up to Darcy.

"I could not see you changing your stripes in this situation, Darce." He smiled at his cousin who returned the grin.

"Thank you, Richard. You saved my life, and I dare say my greatest chance for happiness."

Lord Aubrey entered the conversation at this point. "It has been a long day, gentlemen. I believe I shall call it a night. Darcy, I have sent an express to Agatha, informing her of Elizabeth's safety."

Darcy nodded, adding "I have sent one to Longbourn, and Gracechurch Street as well."

"Good thinking, man," Aubrey said, eyeing Darcy thoughtfully. He approached the man until he was close enough to add, softly. "Thank you, Darcy, on behalf of Agatha and myself. I know not what we would have done if she... if any of them had come to harm." He could continue no longer, as both men looked at each other, knowing they would die in defense of Elizabeth and her children.

"Thank you, sir." Both nodded, and Aubrey made for the door. Darcy drained his glass and said, "I believe I shall follow Lord Aubrey's example, gentlemen, and call it a night. Colonel McGuire?" he nodded to the commander, than to his cousin, "Fitzwilliam."

"Goodnight, Darcy," responded both soldiers. Colonel Fitzwilliam continued. "I will wake you in the morning."

"Ah, perhaps not in the early hours, cousin. I believe I may sleep in, then see if I may be of service to Eli... to the Duchess and the boys."

"Of course," Colonel Fitzwilliam replied, trying to maintain a straight face. Darcy glowered at his cousin to no avail. The man's lips twitched upward as Darcy turned and left the room.

~ CHAPTER ELEVEN ~

June, 1812
Reston Village, Essex

Darcy knocked lightly half-expecting her to be already asleep. He was heartened when Elizabeth cracked open the door. Seeing Darcy's face, she smiled and his fatigue left him instantly. He quickly entered and as she shut the door, she leaned her back against it. He looked at her, unexpectedly overcome with shyness. She stood only in her shift, her hands clasped, one running along the slender fingers of the other. Her nervousness calmed his agitation. His chuckle caused her to look at him, questioningly.

Taking a quick glance around the room, he noted with satisfaction that the adjoining room was barred by a closed, and he hoped locked door. He loved her boys, but did not wish them claiming their mother this night. Satisfied, he focused his gaze back on Elizabeth. Tentatively, he stepped closer to her, raising his hand so it's back caressed her cheek, tears moistening his eyes, as his fingers gently dusted the discolored skin. Her eyes challenged his as she pressed his hand softly onto her skin. When she released the pressure, turning her lips into his palm, his delight completely subdued his fear. Slowly her eyes lifted to his and he saw confusion, gratitude, relief and fatigue, but deep within there was something he could not comprehend. He stood longer than he realized looking into those deep pools he had dreamt of for so long. He saw her strength, and her need to be reassured, and 'God help me, it is enough.' Rapidly, he moved to embrace her, pulling her into his body. The sensation of her melting into him was beyond comprehension. Never before had he felt such gratitude as he did holding her in his arms. 'Finally,' he thought, 'she needs me as much as I need her.' As her lips met his skin he strangled the last ounce of fear that whispered, 'but for how long?'

Elizabeth's hands actively caressed him, helping him remove his jacket, waistcoat and cravat. Before his brain could catch up with the maddening sensations she engendered in him, he felt his shirt being pulled from his breeches, and soon he was lost to thought all together as her fingers danced on the bared expanse of his chest. His moan stilled her movement, and he looked down into her eyes, now dancing with delight. The image of her arched brow, and passion glazed eyes seared into his brain before he crushed his lips to devour hers.

He walked them towards the bed, never releasing her. His hands quickly divested her of her gossamer shift. He pulled away, his hands on her arms holding her so he could drink in the details of her form. His eyes darkened at the purple splotches that marred her waist, and he gently brushed over them. She winced momentarily and stilled. Breathing deeply, she took hold of his hands, guiding them slowly to her breasts. Darcy had difficulty maintaining his composure as she pressed his hands over her mounds, rubbing his thumbs over her puckering nipples. She gasped and it undid him. Reclaiming her lips, he pulled her against him, rubbing her naked body into him, both lost in the other.

Darcy scooped her in his arms, gently laying her on the bed. While she settled onto the pillows, he fumbled with his boots, and breeches, tossing them both in a tangled heap toward the middle of the room. Although he wanted to be gentle with her, his need, her need was too strong. Her scent was upon him and he needed to stake his claim that she was and would always be his.

~

The next morning, Colonel McGuire joined the London party at the inn. He was more than pleased to find her Grace at the breakfast table, conversing with apparent ease with Lord Aubrey. Accustomed to interrogating officers in his command, he was unsure how to obtain the information his curiosity sought. As he settled into his chair, assessing the woman sitting across from him. 'She looks calm enough.' Recalling the details Darcy had provided the evening before, Elizabeth rose even higher in his esteem. Turning to see the puppy dog eyes of the legendarily taciturn Fitzwilliam

Darcy gazing adoringly at the beautiful woman, McGuire chuckled inwardly. 'Better to not even entertain such thoughts. She is as good as at the altar.' He stole another glance at Elizabeth assuring himself that she was recovering from her ordeal. After taking a needed sip from his cup of coffee, he began, "Your Grace, if it is not too distressing, how did you make your escape…? I admit to an overwhelming curiosity regarding your capture, but I confess to being exceptionally curious as to how you eluded him."

She swallowed the last mouthful of her muffin before responding. "I was taking the boys to…" she turned to Darcy, then lowered her eyes quickly. Instantly his mind screeched to a halt. 'She was coming to me when… Wickham…' His fork dropped to his plate, his thoughts a tumble as guilt washed over him suffocating all else. Fitzwilliam and McGuire exchanged nervous glances with Aubrey before all three returned their eyes to the stricken Darcy. He felt a cold chill run through his body, separating him from the world. He felt himself quake, as self-loathing rippled through him. A slight pressure on his thigh spread a steady heat upward to his chest. With considerable effort he looked down where her hand was gently massaging his leg. He lowered his hand over hers and turned it to clasp his in protective warmth. Finally he was able to look her in the eye and he felt his breath return. He found love and compassion in her eyes and he found the strength to calm himself. He nodded and she resumed her tale.

"Wickham stopped my carriage, his men had replaced my driver and footmen. As I was about to scream, a handkerchief covered my face and then..." her face reflected the horror and confusion of not knowing exactly what had happened after that. The men regretted exposing her to such torment. After a moment, she was able to continue. "The next thing I recall was waking with my children, the three of us in that barren room in a neglected house in the middle of nowhere.

"The first night he left us completely alone... in the dark. The next day, he tried to... insinuate himself... I resisted and he... became violent." She paused deciding how much to reveal. The men's reactions decided her course. "I came to... no lasting harm... only a bruise or two before convincing him it would serve his purpose better if he... refrained from any contact... of a ... a more physical nature."

The sound of ripping linen jolted everyone from the dark corners of their thoughts. Colonel Fitzwilliam put a steadying hand on his cousin. Elizabeth continued, "By the third day I had healed enough to contemplate our escape. I began to look around. Out of the window I saw a piece of metal hanging from the roof. When I pulled on it, a good sized piece, about yea long," she indicated with her hands the length of pipe "came off in my hand. Wickham returned near evening. I hid along the wall, and when he opened the door, I hit him with it from behind. His gun, he had a gun... I was afraid of what he would do to the boys..." She began to cry and Darcy drew his arms around her heedless of the looks crossing the faces of Lord Aubrey and the colonels. When she was able, Elizabeth continued. "I hit him again and he fell. The gun discharged when it hit the floor, and then," she lowered her voice to a whisper, so the three men gathered closer. "I felt such rage run though me," she looked at each man in turn. "For what he had done to me, and my family, I struck him, repeatedly, with my fists." She took a deep breath, her eyes now lowered as well. She began to weep, sobs shaking her body. "The gun, the noise, my boys…" she looked up at Aubrey. "That he might harm them… I do not know what came over me, but I could not stop. I just hit him again and again until I could hit no more."

Lord Aubrey leaned back. His movement caught her eye. He nodded at her and she felt absolved.

"When I left, he still breathed. It was as if I woke from a dream, and he lay there on the floor. I feared I had taken his life, but he still breathed."

"Good girl," Aubrey said, impressed with her composure.

"I ripped my petticoat, and bound his arms, behind his back and we fled. There were two horses and the cart he must have brought us in, in the stable. I saddled the horse, as best I could, and we rode out to the wood. I thought that would be safest. I remembered what Rafael told me, that when lost, find a stream and follow it. *'Follow it downstream, Lizzy,'* he would say. *'Always downstream.'* So I did. But the boys, sleep overcame them and both almost escaped my grasp. Trying to save them, I let the horse mind her way, and she stumbled. That is where you found us." Darcy looked at her and smiled. She looked up into his eyes and felt her heart open and taste freedom.

~

Immediately upon their return to London, Elizabeth departed for Crystalglen, taking Agatha and Jane with her. She wanted to give herself and her children the chance to heal, away from the curiosity of London society. She had been gone two weeks before Wickham's trial was over and Darcy felt he could, in good conscience return to her. He, Lord Aubrey and Richard Fitzwilliam had exerted all their substantial influence to see the trial was swift, severe and as secret as possible. That Wickham had sought revenge against a peer of the realm involved a certain amount of notoriety, but money was exchanged in the effort to keep the Duchess' name out of the papers.

However, not all mention could be avoided, and word of the recent misfortune made its way to the gossip dens frequented by Caroline Bingley and her ilk. Piecing together the bits of information she gleaned listening at doors when Mr. Darcy discussed 'those Bennets' with her brother, she had enough to fabricate quite a story for her friends. Dispersing fragments in well placed ears increased her value as a social companion, and she found her calendar full of invitations from the first circles of society. On many such occasions, she noted that Lord Vreeland was present and most eager to hear what she had to tell.

"Miss Bingley, a pleasure to see you again," the affable man began one evening at the home of the Countess Delaney.

Noting the well dressed man to his left, Caroline Bingley dropped her gaze demurely and offered her hand, which Vreeland eagerly took in his. He bowed before introducing his companion, Viscount Amery de Wither.

"Lord de Wither, I am honored to make your acquaintance."

"As am I, Miss Bingley. I have heard much of you." While she blushed like an ingénue, both men exchanged glances of another sort.

"I hear that *you* are a most reliable source of information regarding the recent… escapades…?"

"You would accuse me of gossip, Lord Vreeland," her catty smile countered the affronted tone of her delivery.

"Not at all. We, Vreeland and I are… were good friends of the late Duke…" de Wither added.

Caroline nearly snorted. "His Grace must be turning in his grave!" she sneered. "To have someone so low born cavorting about with the likes of …"

Vreeland and de Wither were alarmed at the acrimony of her words. Caroline's face was contorted with rage, her eyes filled with venom. Vreeland continued, "As you say, Miss Bingley. But we can only hope that, for the sake of… the children… that this unpleasantness will fade from speculation?" As she looked up into his eyes, her challenge quickly melted. She saw the steel of his will, and she slowly nodded her acquiescence. Convinced she understood his meaning, Vreeland smiled. "Miss Bingley, at the risk of altering the course of our discussion, I was hoping that you and perhaps your brother might join me for dinner next week? I find myself in want of good company, and am arranging a little dinner party to make up for the lack of… interesting conversation of late."

"While I would be more than happy to attend, I am afraid my brother is unavailable."

"Oh?" asked de Wither.

"Yes," Caroline huffed. "He and Mr. Darcy travel to Crystalglen… to be of service to the Duchess and her sister."

"Ah!" de Wither beamed.

"Perhaps another evening, then?"

Unwilling to lose the connection, Caroline boldly spoke. "However, my sister, Mrs. Hurst and her husband may be available."

Reluctantly appraising her for her boldness, Vreeland offered, "Then I shall amend my invitation to include them. Until next week, then?" Vreeland left the duo to converse. He chuckled slightly as he met another acquaintance, setting up a rendezvous for later that night.

~

Crystalglen

Darcy hurried through his bath, eager for a private moment with Elizabeth. They had not had another opportunity to indulge their declarations of love, and he was both eager and nervous to see her, to probe her heart that her affections remained unchanged.

Seeing his agitation, Agatha took mercy on her favorite, directing him to the apple grove she knew Elizabeth favored. He found her there, apple blossoms adorning her curls, the light streaming through her gown. His body reacted immediately; his heart raced while his blood pooled in his loins. Stepping forward, a twig snapped, and she turned instantly.

"Mr. Darcy?" her smile reassured him of his welcome.

"Your Grace," he quickly closed the distance, until he stood two feet away, his body leaning forward eagerly. She offered her hand to him, which he gladly took to his lips. Instead of releasing it, he wrapped his free hand over it, capturing and bringing her hand toward his chest. Her eyes flared wide, as she watched him rub her hand against his body. Seeing her reaction, he stilled his movements. "Forgive me if I presume too much, madam." He lowered his hand, but could not release it.

Sensing his vulnerability, Elizabeth looked quickly up into his eyes. "No, no, it is not that, sir. I am… overcome!" She looked away, and then returned her gaze to meet his. "So much has happened, has it not? Our feelings, my feelings have undergone such a change…"

"Do you… do you regret?" A thought suddenly ran through his mind. "There is… Elizabeth, is there any… development from our…?" His voice dropped to a whisper.

She blushed, pleased with his phrasing. "Yes," she whispered. He gasped and she hurriedly continued. "But not… of *that* nature."

Relief washed over his handsome features. Taking the hand he still clung to, he pulled her closer, yet still outside of his embrace. "Then what, my love?" She pulled away, needing distance to order her thoughts. His hopes began to dwindle. "You do not… do you… regret…?"

"Do you?" she had turned, fear gripping her heart.

"NO! Not even if… you do… That night was the most precious moment of my life."

Elizabeth advanced to him, both hands open and reaching for him. She took his hands in hers bringing them to her lips she kissed each one, repeatedly. His heart flew open and he embraced her, his lips crushing hers.

"Elizabeth! I love you." His kisses moved from her lips, to her cheek, her neck, her hair. "I have never felt such love." He pulled away to look at her. "When I heard you were gone, I felt such shame, for abandoning you. I am so sorry. I beg your forgiveness." His eyes were full of the emotion roiling in his heart. She saw him, heard the vulnerability as he humbled himself before her. He pulled back, his hands running down her arms to clasp her hands once again. "I… was afraid, Elizabeth… that you would be harmed, and the fault was mine. I knew then, I would not rest until you were safe."

She looked up at him, processing all he was saying, all that was left unsaid. "When I heard your scream, I was grateful that at least you were alive, and near. That you held me… allowed me to hold you… to defend you… if… if things had progressed differently I would have died a happy man seeing the love I found in your eyes. To find later… more than welcome…" he smiled, unable to mar the joy of those moments. "That you loved me," his voice became a whisper, full of reverence and awe. "Your love is beyond words, my heart." He looked into her eyes, his soul bare to her, and she shivered. Her hands held his tight, and a smile, innocent and full spread over his face. Suddenly his eyes dropped to their hands, clasped together. Shyly he looked up. "Elizabeth, I am not worthy to ask, but my heart says I must." He stepped forward, then rocked back, his weight shifting back to one foot. "Will you… is it possible you could… will you have mercy on me, and be my life… I mean wife?" He blushed at his faux pas.

Looking up, he saw her smile radiating from her eyes. His face lit with joy and he opened his arms to her. She eagerly stepped in and he wrapped himself around her, lifting her in his delight. He felt her gentle hands push against his chest, and he lowered her to the ground to force his thoughts away from the carnal desire that shot through him. She stepped back, looking up at him, her eyes still beaming with love.

"Yes, Fitzwilliam, I shall be your wife. Not only do my boys need you in their lives, but I find that I need you." Her cheeks blushed crimson. "You… have shown me a new side of yourself… one you have kept hidden for so long." He blushed at her words.

"Was I… am I… is my love so hard to accept?" he asked in a whisper.

"Sometimes… it is." Her arms embraced her waist. "When Rafael declared his love."

Darcy turned away. "Please, spare me comparing *my* feeble attempts of lovemaking to the prowess of Rafael Gainsbridge!"

Taking umbrage of his disparaging the dead, she declared, "No, I will not spare you. You *must* understand how… why I have hesitated in accepting *my* love for you."

Her words had their desired affect, he stopped, stunned at her declaration.

"I love you, Fitzwilliam, with a love so overwhelming, so fierce it frightens me." He had taken her arms in his hands, holding her as if she would dissolve, or escape. "Yours is not a love that will accept half measures." Darcy wondered if that were true for he was starving for anything from her. But she continued. "You are not one who may be ignored, or pushed away. You, your love demands all of me, and this… for so long this frightened me. With Rafe I was a young wife for so brief a moment. Then, his illness demanded I become nursemaid as well as lover. Then mother and now… widow." She tore her eyes from him to scan the gravel of the path, trying to compose the sea of emotion rolling through her. "I regret nothing, for those moments with him were precious, but they left me… empty inside." She returned her gaze to him as her eyes searched his. She continued. "Then you came to me, offering a different kind of love all together; a healthy, strong, encompassing love that fills me completely. One that offers the world yet threatens to consume me."

His eyes bore into her, until he could probe her depths no longer. Finally, he looked away, his hands releasing her. He was broken. She grabbed hold of him. "All I have ever asked of you was time. Time to acclimate myself to this new reality."

He quickly returned his eyes to hers, begging silently for more. She obliged. "When you came for us… for me… I knew there was no backing down."

"I do not want your gratitude, Elizabeth." His head hung low.

"It is not gratitude, Fitzwilliam." He looked at her, testing her truth. "You put your life at risk for me. If you were willing to make that… sacrifice… I realized I must be brave enough to risk… my heart… once more."

As her words penetrated his being, Darcy felt himself crumble. He staggered and she caught him. Rather than release her, he pulled her to him, kissing her incessantly. In between his kisses which were mingled with hers, he begged, "Marry me, Elizabeth! Please, say you will be mine!"

When able, she replied, "Yes, my heart, I am yours, I will marry you and share all your tomorrows..." Whatever else Elizabeth was about to say Darcy cut off as he redoubled his attack upon her lips, ears and neck. She laughed in delight until she moaned. The light in his eyes was blinding and Darcy relaxed into his fate for the first time in years. His smile was wide and full and he picked her up and twirled her around. Her laughter, soon joined by his, filled the grove. Slowly he slid her down his body, her feet lightly touching the ground. His eyes darkened, his nostrils flared as his arms pulled her to him.

She felt his arousal, her blood rushing to her own. Her arms tightened around him, and she offered him her lips. He took them and his body eclipsed his mind. His hands held her hips to his and the friction caused them both to moan. Soon he was gathering her skirts, and she, undoing the buttons of his breeches. With her skirts hitched about her waist, he raised her legs, so they clasped about his hips, and he fell to his knees. He pulled back from her mouth to look into her eyes. The welcome he found there released his heart and he smiled. He then laid her on the grass, beneath the blossoming orchard trees, and they made their way to their bliss.

~

When they returned to the manor, they found their family and friends gathered in the music room.

Georgiana was at the pianoforte, Jane and Bingley sitting together, speaking in low tones. With the boys staying close to her, Agatha surveyed the scene, contented with the peace finally settled in her home. As Darcy and Elizabeth entered the room, the music stilled, conversation ceased, and six pairs of eyes eagerly looked at the blushing couple.

Rising with her hands folded in front of her, Agatha spoke as the boys ran to their mother. "Well," she looked at one then the other of the stammering newcomers. "Have you anything to say for abandoning us so suddenly? Darcy? Elizabeth?" She tried very hard to suppress the smile threatening to undo her severe matriarchal pose.

Clearing his throat, he looked at his beloved. Her eyes sparkled in delight. Turning to address the company, Darcy spoke, "Yes, indeed I do, madam." He looked to Elizabeth. "I should say, we do. Elizabeth has done me the supreme honor of agreeing this day, to be my wife!"

The clamor of joy that surrounded them was deafening. Georgiana squealed while scooping Rafael in her arms while Jane took Ian in hers, tears of happiness streaming from her eyes as she embraced her sister with her free arm. Bingley clapped him on the back offering his sincere congratulations. Looking between his friend and his future sister, Darcy added, "Perhaps we will be brothers before long?" Bingley had the grace to blush, but nodded in approval. Darcy laughed and clasped his friend on the shoulder. Agatha ordered champagne and soon they were toasting to love and happiness for all. While Elizabeth and Darcy's eyes were bright, no one ignored the shy glances between Jane and Bingley, their smiles sending wordless messages.

~ CHAPTER TWELVE ~

August, 1812
Pemberley, Derbyshire

Laughter filtered through the open windows and doors of the ballroom as Fitzwilliam Darcy led his betrothed, Elizabeth Bennet Gainsbridge, Duchess of Deronshire to the dance floor. Their relatives and friends gathered around celebrating the approaching wedding. No expense was spared in making the event a spectacular success. Agatha and the Bennets were resplendent in new gowns and full smiles. While not officially *out* Georgiana was allowed to attend and dance with her relations and the close friends of her brother while Catherine and Lydia were effectively sidelined, as being too young to dance with anyone save their father and Uncles Gardiner and Philips. Even so, they found ample amusement flirting with the available young gentlemen called to the wilds of Derbyshire for the ball.

While initially vociferous in disparaging the union, Lady Catherine de Bourgh had at last, and after long discussions with her daughter, brother and sister-in-law, agreed to attend, sanctioning the union. Anne de Bourgh was ecstatic with the betrothal of her cousin to another, as this cleared the path for her to claim her own happiness. Under the guise of improving her mind and chances of enticing her intellectual cousin, Anne had attended one or two of the Gainsbridge salons when the Duke was alive. There she had encountered the Viscount Amery de Wither.

Lord de Wither was a bookish sort of man, with an ironic outlook, one that surprisingly well matched his beloved. Once Darcy's engagement was announced, Lord de Wither sought and won the hand of Anne de Bourgh. Lady Catherine was a bit more difficult to convince, but coming to Pemberley with an Earl-in-waiting in her pocket did much to soothe her ire. Not wishing to distract any from the happy couple, the new lovers had insisted on waiting to announce their impending union. Their only objection to the delay was being limited to two dances at the fete d'amour.

Caroline Bingley did not recover as gracefully from her loss of the Darcy fortune, but she was not willing to miss the opportunity of displaying herself in front of the eligible and desirable bachelors who would inevitably gather at Pemberley. She had outdone herself, focusing her abundant clothing allowance for the next year towards fashioning a gown demonstrating her ability to display the height of style and taste. She insisted on precious jewels around her neck, drawing attention to her less than abundant décolletage.

As she entered the ballroom, Miss Bingley's appearance was noted by all with varying degrees of interest. Those in need of a fortune took her ridiculous appearance as the sign of an easy mark. The more intrepid, or perhaps desperate, headed in her direction to request a place on her dance card. Much to their disappointment, Caroline dismissed the majority of fortune seekers out of hand, allowing only those with a pedigree or title to lead her to the floor where they often found themselves in proximity to Darcy and the Duchess, or worse, Jane Bennet and Caroline's brother, Charles.

Nearly an hour after the ball began Malcolm Lord Vreeland entered the room, accompanied by Robert Smithers and a young, handsome gentleman. Taking in the surroundings, they quickly found their quest and walked in her direction.

"Miss Bingley, how fortuitous to see you this evening," Vreeland had taken her hand, bringing it almost to his lips. Startled, she remained quiet until the debonair bachelor rose from his slight but proper bow. She calculated his sincerity with the precision of a cobra assessing a mongoose.

"Lord Vreeland, a pleasure to see you again."

He smirked as she peered at her companions before allowing her eyes to dart about the crowd, tallying who witnessed the three rather distinguished looking and very eligible gentlemen paying her court. His gesture expanded to include his companions. "You recall my neighbor, Robert Smithers?"

"Yes, from Surrey, is it not?"

The three gentlemen attempted to hide their smiles. Vreeland spoke first, "Precisely. And this is our good friend Cavendish, Ronald Cavendish."

"A pleasure to see you again, Mr. Smithers, Mr. Cavendish, enchanting to meet you." Caroline tried to school her features into some form of sophistication, but the proximity of so much capital and social prominence focused upon her was weighing heavily upon her composure. The three men exchanged glances, as they aligned themselves to observe the dancers gliding about in front of them.

Lord Vreeland sidled up to Miss Bingley, whispering in her ear. "How advantageous for you, my dear Miss Bingley."

"Advantageous, sir? What is advantageous to me?" said she, irritated at not catching a perceived advantage to herself.

"Why, your brother being so very clever aligning himself with the house of Bennet! Effective, yet so artlessly done, it would seem." The man began to grate on her the more he spoke.

"The house of Bennet, indeed," Caroline snorted. Her companions took in her derision, exchanging knowing looks behind her back.

"Indeed," he delighted in her discomfort. Her self-proclaimed pursuit of Darcy had, over the years, provided ample amusement for Vreeland and his set, who often vacillated between eschewing and embracing women of her ilk. But her single-minded attempt to destroy the name and memory of his dear friend, Rafael

Gainsbridge, one of the few men who looked upon his... predilection... with compassion and tolerance, was beyond him to ignore. "I would think one's social standing could only rise with such a... connection... the house of Bennet to the house of Gainsbridge, to the house of Darcy. Astounding, really..."

Vreeland took in the working of Caroline's mind as she made the social calculations. The avarice practically gleamed through her eyes as they narrowed, and her smile took on an unsettling slant. Catching his school chum Lord de Wither walking away from 'that simpering Anne de Bourgh, and her abysmal mother, Lady Catty,' he returned his attention to the scheming Miss Bingley, a wicked thought developing in his mind. 'That would just be delicious!' he thought. 'And I am starved for a bit of entertainment.' "Ah, there is de Wither."

"Lord de Wither?" she asked, her social senses tingling. 'An amiable man, easily led, I would say, and with enough money to satisfy...hmmmmm.'

"Yes, he was a classmate of mine at Cambridge. Do you know him?" he asked, innocently.

Affronted that he had forgotten their previous conversation where *he* had introduced them, she stalled, attempting to decide how to respond. "We met... by your introduction, sir, once I returned form the wilds of Hertfordshire."

"Poor dear, but what fine hunting your brother enjoyed, what?" he smiled as a cat would address a mouse. "Come, let us go speak with him," he said as he gracefully led Caroline and their companions to Amery's side. As they approached, de Wither spoke first.

"Vreeland! My man, how are you? It has been an age..."

"Yes, yes, quite," replied the social animal. "Amery, you recall Miss Bingley. Miss Caroline Bingley, Viscount Amery de Wither."

"A pleasure, Miss Bingley."

She curtsied before responding, "Indeed, a pleasure, sir."

"If you will excuse me, Miss Bingley, I believe all this dancing," his arm spread out, indicating the overflowing dance floor, "leaves me in need of refreshment. May I bring you back a glass of punch, madam?" Vreeland asked bowing his head before his smirk could be detected.

"That would be delightful, Lord Vreeland. I thank you."

Vreeland, Smithers and Cavendish headed toward the refreshment table. As they passed, Lady Catherine glowered. She had focused her prodigious powers of observation as Vreeland led Caroline Bingley over to de Wither, her presumptive son-in-law. She was not pleased that he was now left with that notorious social climber. Leaving Anne with her brother, the Earl of Matlock, Lady Catherine set her course to determine just what Lord Malcolm Vreeland was up to.

"Miss Bingley, would you join me?" Lord de Wither asked out of politeness as well as unease in being alone with this notorious snob with nothing to do and knowing they shared no common interests.

"Delighted, sir, I thank you," said Caroline Bingley as she took his offered hand, her jaded eye appraising the envy such a distinguished partner engendered in her fellow contenders. She noted with glee the raised fans and covetous glances cast by the huntresses scattered about the room. She glided across the floor in the arms of the blue blooded, if not dashing Viscount. Particularly satisfying was the murderous scowl of Lady Catherine who stood by an unusually large arrangement of flowers. As they swept along the room, Caroline's delight only increased when she caught sight of Anne de Bourgh. 'What a pity, all that fortune and prominence wasted on that… mouse,' Caroline's vindictive gleam nearly faltered as Anne's look of concern turned to a knowing smile. Quickly righting herself, she took in the countenance of her partner. Lord de Wither had the tail end of a smile and Caroline would swear she had seen him wink in the *other* lady's direction. She plastered her smile on tightly, and addressed her partner.

"Are you a friend of the Darcys, sir?" she asked, batting her eyelashes.

"Of their extended family, yes." He took hold of her hand as she danced around him. "In fact I am in debt to him, really."

Caroline's eyebrow raised, an involuntary reaction to the scent of gossip.

"Truly?" her salivary glands went into overdrive.

"Yes," he chuckled about to unleash his tale when he spied Elizabeth and Darcy. Recalling himself, he only added, "Indeed." Following his line of vision, Caroline scowled as she saw Darcy embrace Elizabeth as she swept about his attractive form.

As the final notes of the dance reverberated among the crowd, de Wither led Caroline off to the company of her brother, sister, and Miss Jane Bennet. Wishing to maintain the pretense of an eligible, unengaged gentleman, he quickly asked Miss Bennet to dance. Elizabeth and Darcy again took to the floor, as the melodic and scandalous strains of a waltz flowed through the room.

Another participant on the floor took in the pairing, calculating how he could finagle a dance with the delectable Duchess. As the music ended, he guided his nearly inert, but socially acceptable partner near de Wither and Miss Bennet as they regrouped with Darcy and Elizabeth. A smug smile lit up Vreeland's face as Elizabeth graciously accepted his request for a dance. Although impervious to the allurement of women in general, he admired beauty and elegance and wit, all of which his current partner possessed in abundance.

"It is a shame our paths have not crossed more frequently, your Grace," he said as she came closer to him. When she arched her brow, even he, a *confirmed* bachelor, sensed danger.

"Why so, sir?" she asked and he marveled at the laughter dancing in her eyes.

"I have missed the quality of your salon, madam, and would greatly enjoy revisiting the experience."

When her step faltered and the light dimmed in her eye, Vreeland could have hit himself. "Forgive me, madam, it was thoughtless of me..."

"No, please. My time with the Duke is not to be forgotten. They were years of joy and good company." Elizabeth looked into Vreeland's blue eyes and their sincerity nearly undid him. "Rafe spoke of you often, Lord Vreeland. There were many times... many discussions he had wished you had joined, as... how did he put it? There is no one who can turn about an argument quite like Vreeland. Even Shaugnessy could not stand against him."

Despite his years in society, guarding and promoting his persona of social cynic, Vreeland laughed aloud. "You are a jewel, your Grace. I am happy you have found joy, again, although one would wonder at your choice of *Dour Darcy* for your life's companion."

Glancing at her intended, whose eyes followed the pair around the floor, she smiled his way before returning her fine eyes to Vreeland. "He is not so... dour, sir, once you unleash his inner... boy."

"Indeed? I do believe that may be said for us all, do you not agree?"

"Perhaps. If that is the case, I hope you will join our merry meetings once we return to London."

"It would be my pleasure, madam."

As Vreeland returned Elizabeth to him, Darcy's heart felt free again. "Madam, I believe this is our dance?" he asked, as he took her hand from Vreeland, bringing it to his lips before placing it on his arm.

"I believe you are correct, sir," she smiled at him and they headed for the dance floor, leaving Vreeland a recommitted ally. As the couple spun onto the dance floor Vreeland took a moment to observe Lord Danvers dancing with Georgiana Darcy. He smiled thinking of Darcy's reaction when he espied his sister dancing with such an eligible young man. His reverie was halted as Caroline Bingley returned to haunt him.

"Lord Vreeland," she began.

"Ah, Miss Bingley, how went your hunt... I mean, dance?"

"Well, sir, Lord de Wither is a true gentleman, but does not seem inclined to amiable conversation."

"Patience, Miss Bingley, sure and steady wins the race, so I am told." And with that he sauntered off to an alcove one of his *associates* had indicated was private enough for a bout of *male* bonding.

Composing herself after being abandoned by two eligible members of the first circle, Caroline straightened her spine and looked around for someone else to cleave to. All around her, the splendor of Pemberley displayed in its glory, revealed to her only enemies and disappointment. The *ton* was gathered to celebrate the engagement of Fitzwilliam Darcy and Elizabeth Bennet Gainsbridge, and many in attendance were more than willing to gloat as Caroline's self-promoted claim to the position of the next mistress of Pemberley was exposed as the lie it had always been. Even her brother had abandoned her in his pursuit of the insipid Jane Bennet, sister to the interloper. Caroline sulked over to her own sister, Louisa, in search of some spiritual salve. Instead, she found Mrs. Hurst speaking with a Mrs. Gildcrest, both going on about the benefit of Charles' close association with the house of Bennet.

On the dance floor, the feted couple communicated silently, enjoying the pleasure of their hands upon each other as they waltzed among their guests. Observing his soon-to-be sister dancing with his friend, he remarked, "Your sister and Bingley seem to be well suited, Elizabeth." Darcy still relished every opportunity to address her so intimately.

"Indeed. Their courtship seems well on its way to a happy conclusion." She gasped as he drew her closer to his body.

"Not nearly as happy as our own, my dear."

"You are incorrigible," she laughed, her eyes lost in his. He twirled her around him, his body the axis upon which she revolved. His eyes bore into her as his desire sprung to life causing Elizabeth to blush and avert her eyes. As she did, she witnessed a disconcerting sight. "But what of Lord de Wither?" Her comment directed Darcy's gaze from her exquisite eyes to the man again dancing with Caroline Bingley. Quickly he scanned the sidelines where he found his aunt, who fumed in agitation, while his cousin seemed unperturbed.

"What is he about?" he asked, half to himself.

Elizabeth also watched the de Bourghs unable to comprehend Anne's docile reaction to the near stranglehold Miss Bingley held on her partner's arm. She quickly returned her gaze to Darcy, a questions on her lips. "But I thought..."

"As did we all..." sensing her unease, he diplomatically altered the conversation. "Worry no more about it, my love, all will be well." Her sparkling eyes rewarded him.

"Ever the optimist, are we, Mr. Darcy?" her upturned lips teased his desire. Rather than claim her kiss, he whirled her around as his arms tightened their embrace. They remained in as close proximity as propriety allowed during the brief moments remaining of the ball.

Within days the Bingleys left Pemberley to escort Jane Bennet back to Hertfordshire. After spending three tedious weeks at Netherfield, Caroline anticipated returning to London. She was eager to resume her acquaintance with Lord Vreeland, and was extremely pleased to find an invitation to a dinner at his home, Evermore, awaiting her. Upon arriving she noted to her dismay that Lady Catherine de Bourgh and her daughter, Anne, were in attendance as well. They were civil to the tradesman's daughter, going so far as to introduce her to Count Pleginyev, a diplomat from Russia appointed to the court of St. James. Caroline was pleasantly surprised to find herself nearly the sole point of *his* interest and was thrilled when he invited her for a ride in the park the next afternoon. Caroline even managed to blush becomingly.

Leaving Vreeland's mansion the next morning after a most exhausting night in the arms of his English lover, Pleginyev arranged for the carriage as well as passage back to his home country. He then made haste to keep his appointment with Miss Bingley.

At Bingley House Caroline and her sister, Louisa, were entertaining her brother-in-law, brother and Mr. Edward Gardiner. Even her mortification at being caught with a man of trade in her home as a guest, could not quell Caroline's excitement when Pleginyev handed her in to the carriage, his hand lingering on hers a moment longer than propriety allowed. Settling in to the coach Louisa looked on with anticipation to her role as chaperone. The broad-chested, handsome man presented a dashing figure and 'the attention he pays Caroline is decided, indeed. There is hope after all. He shall certainly help her over the loss of Darcy. If only he didn't have that scar… probably from some duel, or some other exotic pastime and… so manly.' A shiver went up Louisa's spine as she lost herself in thoughts of the alluring Russian telling his tale, in her boudoir on a cold winter's night. As her thoughts evolved, she felt the heat of her blood rise, adding color to her cheek. 'Oh my, what family… reunions there may be…' she thought as the carriage entered the park.

If Louisa was surprised at the Count's greeting the open barouche carrying Lady Catherine and Anne de

Bourgh as well as Amery Lord de Wither, she did her best not to show it. She watched Caroline's reaction closely, relieved that his defection was not ruffling her sister's equilibrium. 'I imagine, a Count in the hand trumps an Earl in the bush, especially,' she noted de Wither's proximity to Anne de Bourgh, 'since his attention appears most decidedly to lie elsewhere.'

Lady Catherine nodded to *that Bingley woman,* satisfied that Sussex's diversion was working. When she had confronted Vreeland at Pemberley he had reluctantly backed off pushing Miss Bingley onto Lord de Wither. Together they had devised a plan ridding their family and friends of the annoying pretensions of Caroline Bingley, without too much of a scandal. Initially skeptical at the plan, she warmed to it as Miss Bingley had vociferously claimed that *she* and not *my sweet Anne* would win de Wither's hand. A wicked gleam lit her eye as their carriage passed out of view.

~ CHAPTER THIRTEEN ~

January, 1813
Pemberley, Derbyshire

The wedding of Fitzwilliam Darcy and Elizabeth Bennet Gainsbridge, Duchess of Deronshire was the social event of the season. The groom was intermittently anxious and giddy as a schoolboy. His nearest and dearest gathered around him to support and celebrate his joining with his beloved.

Elizabeth was resplendent in an ivory gown of the finest silk organza, her curls piled a top of her head, entwined with the delicate flower buds of the creamy yellow that matched those adorning the neck and hemline of her gown. Wearing the Darcy diamond engagement ring, she had placed the Gainsbridge wedding band on her right hand. This had been a point of discussion between Elizabeth, Agatha and Darcy, but Elizabeth and Darcy had prevailed and in honor of Rafael's memory she had kept his presence in place while freeing the appropriate hand to receive the band of gold every Darcy bride had worn for five generations.

While exchanging their vows Elizabeth was struck by how completely she felt each word. 'How much more they bind me to him, and he to me,' she thought as Darcy's rich voice filled Pemberley's Chapel. The autumnal flowers, supplemented by the hot houses of both estates were in abundance around the church. Georgiana and Jane had preceded her down the aisle to meet Charles Bingley and Colonel Fitzwilliam standing by Darcy. Agatha held Ian and Rafael with her having Lydia and Kitty helping to quietly entertain them.

As Elizabeth said, "I do," she felt her heart overflow with love, and she knew she would love the man before her for the rest of her life. And she did.

The newly married Darcys soon found blissful solitude. The carriage ride from the main house to one of the summer cottages situated on the isolated Pember Lake was spent ensconced in loving embraces, where their passion was barely contained. It was only the knowledge that the ride was of short duration that kept Darcy's display in check. After nearly forty-five minutes of exquisite torture, they arrived at the cottage, where provisions were laid in, and they found Mrs. Reynolds there to greet them.

"Mrs. Darcy, Mr. Darcy, how wonderful to welcome you!" she said, tears of joy clouding her vision. The Darcys returned her greeting, their emotions just as accessible. "I have seen to your instructions, sir, and will return with the carriage. I will send Maria in the afternoons, to see to your needs, but otherwise we shall see you next week?"

"Thank you, Mrs. Reynolds. You are a treasure," Elizabeth said, placing her arm on the trusty housekeeper.

"Mrs. Reynolds, as always, I am indebted to your wise administration." Darcy added, kissing her cheek.

The older woman blushed, and not willing to delay the passion she saw in their eyes quickly departed the cottage, taking the driver along with her.

When they were alone, Darcy stood, dumbfounded, looking at Elizabeth. 'She is mine! She is finally mine!' His mind flashed to the first image he had of her, across a ballroom, and his eyes filled with her smile. When she turned, with the same loving smile now offered to him, his feet propelled him and his arms pulled her towards him. Wrapping himself around her, embracing her as if she were life itself, he never wanted to relinquish his hold. His face nestled in the curls atop her head, and the peace he felt filled him with joy. "I love you, Elizabeth. I have always loved you." He murmured in her hair. "Forgive me the times I allowed my jealousy and frustration to pain you."

Elizabeth held him tightly, feeling his vulnerability in every sinew of his strong body. With it, she felt her heart open an unknown chamber, accepting him, loving him more deeply than she had ever imagined possible. It was a love she understood, but a love she had never imagined possible to share with another human soul. It was the state of being she felt in prayer, when she stood before her Creator, honest, bare, whole. That he now stood before her as naked emotionally as she was only able to achieve when facing the Divine humbled her. It deepened her trust in him. As this last door of her heart opened, she revealed her most vulnerable self, and the two, as would innocent children, allowed their love to flare alive, bright and strong enough to fuel their hearts for the rest of their days.

~

Three weeks after the Darcy's marriage, Bingley returned to Netherfield. He called on Longbourn early the day after his arrival. He had come alone, leaving his sister in the able care of Louisa and her husband back in London. After paying the appropriate respects to Mrs. Bennet and the other young ladies of the house, Bingley proposed a walk in the gardens to which Jane Bennet hastily agreed.

"Jane?"

Preoccupied with her hope for the outcome of this discussion, Jane answered in a breathy whisper, "Yes?"

"I..." he stopped them both, boldly taking her hands in his, his thumbs running underneath the kid leather of her gloves. She blushed at the intimacy, daring herself to look up into his eyes. When she did, she found the love and tenderness she had sought all her life. She gasped, glimpsing her future children in his eyes. He continued. "Jane, I have tried to be patient, to give you time to... to come to care for me..."

"I do, Char... Mr. Bingley, I do care for you," she blurted out before drawing one hand to cover her mouth. His smile illuminated him entirely. Seeing him thus, Jane lowered her hand, securing his abandoned one in her own. Her smile mirrored his as he dropped to one knee and asked the eternal words, "Miss Bennet... Jane, will you join your life to mine and be my bride?"

She raised her hands to gently cup his cheek before bending towards him. His gaze never left hers, lifting his face he watched her lips approach, and he licked his own. She pressed her plump lips to his mouth and a shot of pure fire burst through them both. Slowly, he rose, his arms moving to embrace her. Steadying himself, he dragged his arms up to her shoulders pulling her against his body. Her softness met the firm plane of his chest. His hand rode along her back, up her spine, till it cradled her head, repeatedly forcing her lips to his.

"Yes, Charles, oh yes," she cried as her lungs gasped for breath. "I will... I love you so..."

"Jane!" he cried before no more words were spoken for nearly twenty minutes.

∾

The night of Bingley's engagement, Caroline Bingley attended a celebration of another kind. Count Pleginyev had invited her to a very exclusive soiree at the home of the Earl of Bliscomb. She was amazed to find many members of the first circle there, along with more notorious members of the demimonde, all in varying degrees of… diversion. Conversation hummed and she enjoyed herself immensely. Rare caviar, exotic sweets, and cold meats abounded as the hosts knew it would be a very long night. Caroline's glass was never left dry, the fine bubbles of the smuggled French champagne tickled her nose, and when asked how such a rare treat had been found, she was answered with only wry smiles.

At one point, bored with the card tables, she tried escaping the heavy smoke of the cigars the gentlemen were incessantly lighting. She was finding the evening increasingly hilarious. It was past midnight when the Count lured her into the study.

"My dear Miss Bingley," he began leading her into the room. From the shadows, Lord Vreeland, Mr. Smithers and the Earl of Sussex emerged. Caroline swung around, feeling entrapped, as would a fly in the spider's web. Sitting in a chair by the fire, Vreeland lit up a short, stubby cigar. His gaze clung to her through the smoke enwreathing his head. She waved away the acrid smoke as he just sat smiling at her.

"Caroline," the Count crooned in his deep, resonant voice. She startled at his use of her given name. He took her hand, caressing it between his own. "You do not mind if I call you Caroline?" Suspicious, she looked sharply into his eyes, deep dark brown pools that called her in to drown. She nodded her head in agreement. "Good, very good." He looked around the room, silently concurring with his comrades. "We were hoping you would provide... a service... for us."

"Service?" Her defenses instantly rose to the alert. Vreeland rose and moved to the desk that stood against the far wall.

"Yes," drawled the Earl. "My... friends and I are of a mind to enact a bit of the theatrical." The Earl delighted in the gleam of disdain shooting from her eyes.

"And how would I *serve*, sir?" She asked trying to wave away the smoke without looking unsophisticated.

"You would be our... scribe, dear Miss Bingley." Vreeland was at the desk acquiring pen and parchment. "We would be ever so grateful to you if you would."

Taking account of the possibilities of two extremely well suited peers being indebted to her, as well as complying to the delectable Count pushed aside the small clamor of warning growing in her mind. "Of course, sir," she finally said, as she walked over to the desk which Vreeland had prepared for her.

"Excellent!" Vreeland nearly giggled. He pulled the chair for her as Sussex poured a glass of wine, placing it to her left.

"Pray tell, Lord Vreeland, what is the nature of your... drama...?"

Smiling at her as an eagle would before he feeds his victim to his chicks, he said, "it is a scene from a theatrical piece that Sussex and I have worked on infrequently for a year or two. It keeps us... occupied. The scene we shall work on is the part where the hero and heroine discuss the possibility of an... elopement."

"Scandalous!" shrilled Caroline, becoming entranced at being involved in something so lurid.

"Exactly," chimed Smithers. "I shall play the heroine, and Pleginyev here, will play the hero." Caroline looked up in surprise. Laughing slightly he continued, "Fear not, dear lady, we will not offend your maidenly sensibilities."

And so, they began. As she wrote the words the gentlemen twirled about, her mind clouded, becoming as thick as the smoke filled room. The wine and champagne were working on her sensibilities as well. Finally, the gentlemen ceased their theatrical charade, all three crowding around the desk, perusing the sheaves of parchment she had filled. Taking one in his hand, Vreeland requested she re-copy one section in particular.

"This part here, Sussex, is really quite good." Looking up at his companion, he smiled. "Really fine, actually." He turned to the woman whose eyes were growing quite heavy. "Miss Bingley, please forgive us for keeping you so long, but one more… small request and then we shall see you… to your home."

Realizing it would be impossible to refuse, Caroline took the parchment, scanning her writing, stalling as she tried to focus her mind. Vreeland looked over her shoulder. "Here, this section, if you would be so kind as to put it on a fresh, clean sheet, I will be most grateful." His eyes leveled into hers and she nodded. The three observed as she wrote in her best hand the letter they had decided would be sent to their heroine's family informing them of her elopement. When complete, there was a celebratory round of a dark amber liquid that was sweeter than Caroline would have imagined. They conversed a bit, Caroline's mind heavy with fatigue and the inordinate amount of alcohol she had imbibed. Her eyes grew heavy, the smoke from the fire irritated her eyes, but before she faded into oblivion, she saw the fine figure of Count Pleginyev lean down and kiss Malcolm Vreeland.

~

Three days after receiving consent from Thomas Bennet, Bingley received a letter from Louisa announcing that Caroline had eloped with *her dashing young love,* who Louisa could only surmise was Count Pleginyev and that they had sailed for Mother Russia. Unbeknownst to Mrs. Hurst and Mr. Bingley, the Count was only royalty in the demimonde of white slavery and Miss Bingley was quickly transported to the orient, where she was soon immersed in the opium trade. Over time, she worked her way through the treacherous waters of the underworld becoming the prosperous proprietress of an opium den visited by the highest circles of Asian society. She was never heard from again in polite British society. However, British children living in India and China were cajoled into their lessons and keeping their steps to the straight and narrow by threats of falling victim to the Orange Dragon of Shanghai.

~

Jane Bennet became Jane Bingley one brilliant spring day. Elizabeth Darcy was her matron of honor, while Mr. Darcy stood beside his longtime friend as witness to their joy. Lydia, Catherine and Mary Bennet were resplendent in gowns, courtesy of their sisters, while Mrs. Bennet was scouring the groom's guests for suitable prospects for her youngest daughters. Mr. Bennet was able to walk his daughter down the aisle, as he had months before for his favorite, with the use of a cane. As he had for Elizabeth's wedding, Thomas Bennet had a difficult time keeping the tears from clouding his vision.

Although mentioned once or twice during the prewedding festivities, no one truly missed Bingley's other sister, and Louisa relished her unrestrained ability to serve as hostess for her brother's nuptials. As the newly formed Bingleys departed for their honeymoon journey, they sighed with delight of the bliss soon to be theirs.

~ EPILOGUE ~

The Bingleys were happy and content with their lives. Within a year they relocated not thirty miles from Pemberley, as Charles refused to have his mother-in-law disturb the peace of his soon-to-be-born child. They founded their dynasty at Sunnybridge, an aptly named estate for such a sweet tempered couple.

After carefully weighing her options, and following the guidance of her dearest sister to marry only for the deepest love, Georgiana Darcy married her cousin, Richard Fitzwilliam but never had any children of her own. Lord Danvers, who proved to have a wandering eye, was heartbroken, but found consolation three years later with an actress of the opera. The Fitzwilliams moved to France once the continent was again peaceful.

Darcy and Elizabeth enjoyed the rare union of love, passion and mutual respect throughout their married life. While disagreement could not be totally avoided, Elizabeth always found the way to ease the tension in any situation. Darcy found himself at her mercy on every occasion, as even when she was angry at him, he found the fire in her eyes too tempting to resist, and he would woo away her ire. When it came to her, he had no unfounded pride. He needed her; to feel her, love her and have that love returned. When he would look into her eyes, his love exploding into desire, her anger melted, transformed in the heat he created in her heart.

Unsurprisingly, they had five children of their own, in addition to raising Rafael and Ian to adulthood. Darcy loved them as his own, instilling in them, as he did his natural children the love of learning, of family, country and to treat others as you would have them treat you: with integrity, compassion and a touch of tolerance. Their five sons and two daughters all grew surrounded by loving adults, with Dame Agatha, who lived well into her nineties, serving as their surrogate grandmother. When old enough, they all spent a season with their Aunt Georgiana and Uncle Richard in Paris, where they were the darlings of society.

~ ***Fini*** ~

Made in the USA
Lexington, KY
27 January 2011